PENGUIN BOOKS

LISTEN

Sacha Bronwasser is a Dutch writer and art historian. For decades, she worked as art critic for *De Volkskrant*, while also curating exhibitions and writing and speaking about contemporary art for radio, television, and on stage. In 2019, she made her fiction debut with the highly praised novel *Niets Is Gelogen*, followed by the bestselling *Luister* (*Listen*) in 2023 and the short story collection *De Lotgevallen* in 2024. *Listen* was nominated for multiple literary awards, has been translated into several languages, and is currently being adapted into a feature film. Bronwasser lives on the Dutch coast.

David Colmer is the translator of more than eighty book-length works of Dutch-language literature and has won many prizes for his translations, including the International Dublin Literary Award and the Independent Foreign Fiction Prize, both with novelist Gerbrand Bakker.

LISTEN

SACHA BRONWASSER

Translated by DAVID COLMER

PENGUIN BOOKS

PENGUIN BOOKS

An imprint of Penguin Random House LLC
1745 Broadway, New York, NY 10019
penguinrandomhouse.com

The publisher gratefully acknowledges the support of
the Dutch Foundation for Literature.

N ederlands
 letterenfonds
dutch foundation
for literature

Set in Bembo Book MT Pro
Designed by Sabrina Bowers

LIBRARY OF CONGRESS CATALOGING-IN-PUBLICATION DATA

Names: Bronwasser, Sacha, 1968– author | Colmer, David, 1960– translator
Title: Listen : a novel / Sacha Bronwasser ; translated by David Colmer.
Other titles: Luister. English
Description: New York, NY : Penguin Books, 2025.
Identifiers: LCCN 2025005674 (print) | LCCN 2025005675 (ebook) |
ISBN 9780143138464 trade paperback | ISBN 9780593512531 ebook
Subjects: LCGFT: Fiction | Detective and mystery fiction | Novels
Classification: LCC PT5882.12.R66 L8513 2025 (print) |
LCC PT5882.12.R66 (ebook)
LC record available at https://lccn.loc.gov/2025005674
LC ebook record available at https://lccn.loc.gov/2025005675

Printed in the United States of America
1st Printing

Originally published in Dutch as
Luister by Ambo|Anthos Uitgevers B.V., Amsterdam.

The authorized representative in the EU for
product safety and compliance is
Penguin Random House Ireland,
Morrison Chambers, 32 Nassau Street,
Dublin D02 YH68, Ireland,
https://eu-contact.penguin.ie.

LISTEN

Paris, September 2021

THE NEWS TRAVELED FAST; news like that does.

I knew you had been caught up in it the moment the first reports came in from Paris. Almost six years ago now, on a Friday the thirteenth. A date like a bad joke.

All sorts of people checked in online as "safe." Friends, a niece, a distant relative. People I'd studied with, my own former students. Exhibitors from the photo show, your fellow photographers. Others, vague acquaintances; I was surprised how many people I knew on the fringe of a world event. You were there too, Flo, and your profile stayed silent. Ominously silent, as they say.

That night and in the days that followed I studied the videos and news photos. I scrolled through dozens of shots of toppled chairs at sidewalk cafés, floors covered with shattered glass, people in space blankets being carried away on stretchers improvised from crush barriers. Pictures of ambulances and fire engines stranded at odd angles, clusters of police cars. The boulevards, avenues, and squares were packed with first responders, but everything was in short supply.

Was this the place and hour? Was that your hair? Were they your long limbs? Your boots? Would I recognize you after all these years, in this setting?

Were you still alive? That was what I should have asked myself first, of course.

. . .

"LOOKING AND SEEING AREN'T the same thing," you taught us long ago when we were still so young. Me, not even twenty; you, not yet thirty. The classroom wasn't darkened like it usually was. You, our instructor, weren't going to whip up our enthusiasm for a photographer's body of work or the history of the first image, not going to take us on an expedition with a glass plate camera that was being lugged to a distant corner of the world to record the view for the first time in the history of the universe.

No, you were going to teach us what comes first, before the photograph. And you were going to do it close to home. The classroom we had been gathering in at a fixed time each week was, at best, a place we had looked at occasionally but probably never seen. It was now going to be our starting point. You asked us to let our eyes roam for fifteen minutes while mentally naming everything. Only after that quarter of an hour had elapsed were we allowed to take notes; as an exercise it was childishly simple.

We did as you asked, we did everything you asked. Back then, ten years' seniority was the difference between duckling and swan. You sat in silence the whole time, staring out through the window, your sharp profile lit by the low autumn sun. With your boots on the table; it was the eighties.

We'd been coming here for months and only now did I notice how everything in the classroom—from the sagging venetian blinds with their grimy cords to the weary ceiling panels—hung listlessly. Dusty cobwebs were swaying in the air between the fluorescent lights. We saw and named it all silently, from the gleam on the old lino floor (mustard, dented) to the discolored cornices. Everything condensed and then etched itself into memory like the light on one of the daguerreotypes you had told us about a few classes earlier. To this day I can still list those neutral, completely unexceptional details, even the faded cards in the metal slots on the filing cabinet in the corner, sixteen drawers high—and I understood what you were trying to achieve. Someone who sees can tell. And someone who can tell records. We need language to guide our eyes.

Only later did I realize that despite everything that happened, whatever reason you had for choosing me, whoever was guilty of what, it was still you who taught me how to be so observant.

AT FIRST, I WAITED. After the attacks, I waited. I soon heard that you had survived. Also how and what and where, messages came whooshing in. But I waited for more. For Kairos, who reveals the right moment. For courage. Or maybe I was waiting until I'd forgotten you again. So much time had already passed.

But then, in the fall of 2021, that night in Paris returned to screens everywhere. Again those streets, the flashing lights, the dull bangs. The stories. The men involved in the attacks had gone on trial and the French newspapers I read so I can discuss them in class with my students were filled day after day with the testimonies of bystanders and survivors. They even turned it into a Netflix series.

I didn't see your face among the talking heads. Your story wasn't told; you've always remained silent. Again, those images, but you will never see them.

I TOOK SOME LEAVE, came to Paris, and I'm still here.

Where else could I tell this story? I had you to thank for this city. And you me. Paris had inadvertently become the pivot we both turn on. Here I would find the words—for me and for you.

I rode one of those gray self-service bikes down familiar streets to all the addresses I knew by heart. I followed the Seine far beyond the city limits; everything seemed to have shrunk.

I also rode to the locations of the attacks, which I had marked on a map. A wobbly red line. And that was the route I followed yesterday afternoon on the warm asphalt of the empty Boulevard Voltaire; it was the car-free Sunday.

COMPTOIR VOLTAIRE NO LONGER exists. The red awnings have been replaced with blue ones. (Did you see that they were red? Did you name the color?) The brasserie is now called Les Ogres. Meat is still the specialty.

I stood on the sidewalk for a while trying to evoke that Friday, trying to find you in this place. That was still beyond me and I rode on. On the other side of the city, Parisians and visitors were thronged around the Arc de Triomphe, which was wrapped in shiny silver fabric, a posthumous art project by Christo and Jeanne-Claude. It looked like an altar, surrounded by people taking selfies.

Maybe there was nothing under the material. There hadn't been anything there in 1810 either, when the time came for Marie-Louise to ride under the arch and into the city; the construction work had come no further than the foundations. Napoleon had a trompe l'oeil of the Arc painted for her benefit, canvas on a wooden frame, a life-size illusion. She rode under an arch of air and flapping linen. If there's anywhere history is being continuously reappraised, rewritten, and believed again, Flo, if only for a moment, this is it.

I'm sending you these messages from here in Paris. Our story was a pebble in my shoe I'd done my best to ignore, but once it made its presence felt, that was no longer possible. You'll have to make time for it too.

Listen.

I

Philippe's Story

1986

I NEED A THIRD person for our story because every story rests on three points. Otherwise, it falls over. The three points are you, me, and Philippe Lambert. A man I knew only briefly and you not at all, but without him this story can't be told. I don't need to explain to you, Flo, that it's also less awkward for me to have someone else to talk about.

You and I get to spend the coming period outside ourselves, in neutral territory, with him. A character cobbled together from memories and recovered scraps of paper. Assumptions, reconstructions. Rumors, paintings, snippets from other people's stories. Shirts to iron, unfinished sentences, coffee grounds in a cup, cigarette butts in a small ashtray on a staircase. And dates and coordinates. Those too, of course.

Philippe.

EVERY FAMILY HAS A child who's "a bit different," and with the Lamberts it was the youngest. The first three, two boys and a girl, all displayed the self-assured, determined traits of the paternal side from an early age. They were born in Rue Leclerc in the 14th arrondissement in 1948, 1949, and 1951 respectively.

Every morning at quarter past eight, the white tires of a Traction Avant glided up to the curb and the driver waited until

father and director general Christian Lambert had emerged from
the building, opened the rear door (making the driver get out to do
it was too old-fashioned), and lowered himself into the back seat
while taking the hat off his head in a single flowing movement. In
1952 he had been named chairman of the board at the Ministry of
Telecommunication; the culmination of a steady march through the
French civil service. Considered a dandy and a moderate modernist,
he steered clear of politics. In the turbulent waters of the Fourth
Republic, the period without General de Gaulle, it was essential for
La Poste to plow on like a reliable steamboat—M. Lambert had a
predilection for similes.

Essentially the pinnacle for a French civil servant, his new position called for a larger home in a better neighborhood. He settled
on a spacious, horseshoe-shaped apartment with five bedrooms, a
library, and a salon with tall windows, located in Rue Marbeau on
the edge of the fashionable 16th arrondissement, with various
embassies and the German consulate around the corner. The green
haze of the Bois de Boulogne was visible at the west end of the
street, on the other side of the Périphérique.

This step also called for a fourth child.

PHILIPPE'S ARRIVAL ON A February morning in 1954 proceeded so
swiftly that there was no time to make it to the hospital. His
mother, Ghislaine Lambert, gave birth in the foyer on the new parquet floor; the doctor who had been alerted by telephone had just
stepped through the door and still had his coat on.

The new baby was healthy but high-strung, he cried a lot and
had a lazy eye. In his first months he suffered convulsions that made
him jerk his arms and legs wide. The child outgrew this but seemed
permanently on guard and easily upset. For the first five years it
was impossible to leave him alone. He held on tight to the nannies'
aprons and his mother's couture dresses. She was convinced Philippe's
birthplace was to blame. They should never have moved.

During the Exposition Universelle of 1889 this area had been home to a bullfighting arena financed by a consortium of Spanish bull breeders. La Gran Plaza de Toros, an enormous metal-roofed, brick construction, could seat twenty-two thousand spectators. Matadors were brought in from Madrid, the cheering from the arena rang out over the streets, and the ladies of the neighborhood suddenly began appearing with fans and mantillas and carrying signed photographs of El Gordito in their handbags. But after just four years, the Iberian fever had passed. Due to a lack of interest, the building was demolished and the block that came free was filled with Haussmannian apartment buildings.

According to his mother, that arena from more than half a century ago explained Philippe's character. "On this ground," Ghislaine said regularly, pointing at the polished parquet, "too much violence has been committed. Blood has been spilled. A child feels that." This annoyed his father, who said, "We live on the fourth floor, darling. And our first three children were practically born on the catacombs. It never bothered them." In any case, is there an inch of Paris that hasn't been drenched in blood?

It could only be coincidence that his youngest son was a little different. More sensitive, on a less steady keel. Nothing to worry about. He was sure to be smart enough, they all were, and if not, Director General Christian Lambert had the right contacts to ensure that Philippe too landed on his feet.

In the four paintings made of the family over the years, you don't notice anything untoward at all. Philippe's left eye, which continued to droop despite all the expensive treatment, was retouched. All in all, he became quite a handsome boy, with straight chestnut hair he would later pass on to his sons, a very slight stoop, and the angular Lambert jaw that lends itself so well to being captured in oils.

—

WHEN PHILIPPE WAS THIRTEEN his grandmother was hit by a bus and killed while leaving Parc Monceau. Without warning, she had tried to cross Boulevard de Courcelles and the bus, which was coming from the left, had been unable to stop in time. She was a sparrow of a woman and the distraught driver picked her up and sat down on the side of the pavement with her on his lap, a pietà in uniform. Grandmother hadn't suffered; she died instantly.

For days beforehand, Philippe had been restless, not wanting to go to school, hardly eating. He kept saying that Mamie was getting too old to live on the other side of the city, in fact she was getting too old to carry on living alone, couldn't they let her move in with them? His brothers and sister had reached an age at which they found grandparents irritating. They avoided Sunday dinners, gushed about Serge Gainsbourg to annoy their parents, and smoked Afghani black in the deserted servants' rooms on the eighth floor. Their youngest brother was excluded from this pact and adored his grandmother. His parents thought he shouldn't make such a fuss. That morning, he hadn't wanted to leave the house, but his father had taken him with him in his official car and watched to make sure he went through the gates of his strict private school. A few hours later the family received the telephone call.

"Philippe had a premonition," they whispered at the funeral. "He was very close to his grandmother. There's a child like that in every family."

THEIR GREYHOUND'S SUDDEN DEATH from food poisoning in 1971; the zinc plate that crashed down onto the sidewalk just outside their front door after a heavy storm and came within a hair's breadth of crushing the concierge; a fire in the Galeries Lafayette, where his mother was shopping at the time—in retrospect Philippe was quite often scared of things that ended up happening. But sometimes he also got wound up about events that never took place at all. Once, on the way to a weekend in their country home on the coast, already three quarters of an hour outside Paris, he begged his father to go back home, convinced that a pipe had burst in the building. The water was sure to be dripping through the floors. His panic in the car was so tangible that Ghislaine talked her husband into turning back. At home they found a peaceful apartment behind closed shutters. When they set out again for Saint-Valery-en-Caux an hour later, Philippe immediately fell asleep in the back seat, exhausted.

There were places in the city he gave a wide berth: bridges, stations, cemeteries. He could only sleep with the curtains open, ate his meals clockwise, and refused to let the housekeeper polish his shoes, insisting on doing it himself. Words like *compulsion*, *obsession*, and *anxiety* were carefully avoided—the Lamberts did not suffer from things like that. A little sensitive, perhaps. *Un peu nerveux.*

Before he started economics at university, his parents sent him to a psychologist who recommended relaxation therapy, a fairly new phenomenon at the time. He learned to breathe with his stomach and discovered that he could rationalize away fears, ignoring them, sometimes even laughing them off. And also that nobody wanted to hear his warnings. In his circles, self-confidence was the norm. Adversity, failure, fate—they were all for other people. Even the war hadn't changed the family's fortunes, although the details of that were something they didn't talk about. "Always remember, Philippe," his father said, "people like us help the country to advance. We direct the flow of money. We head factories and laboratories. We're responsible for the development of the Concorde and the first European space launch. These things don't happen by themselves: all those trains that run, all those hospitals . . . Think of the hundreds of thousands of people who get onto their bicycles and climb into their yellow vans in the name of La Poste to ensure that all that information ends up where it's supposed to be"—the image of an army of anonymous functionaries moved Philippe's father deeply, he used it every year in his New Year's speech at head office—"these are great processes, wheels that keep society turning, and yes, yes, people like us are behind them. We bring forth leaders, managing directors, what am I saying—presidents. There is no room for doubt. Be a man."

Philippe slid a lock of hair in front of his left eye and did what was asked of him. Apparently, that was possible. Apparently, you could stuff your fears into a mental box and screw down the lid. They were still there, but you grew around them. That also made them invisible to others, who weren't interested in them anyway. He'd learned that.

He completed his studies, obtained a management position with Renault, and, on one of his first business trips to Germany, met Laurence, a meticulously coiffured Air France stewardess. She could spot a passenger with flight anxiety in seconds; it was quite common in first class. A little personal attention could make the trip so much more comfortable. She remained standing in the aisle with the coffeepot in one hand and conversed with Philippe until they commenced descent. There was something appealing about the clammy face turned up toward her and she decided to breach company protocol by asking for his card.

Thanks to their slight figures, straight dark brown hair, and somewhat reticent gait, they could already have been mistaken for family. Laurence brushed over her frugal childhood in Compiègne; Philippe didn't mention his fears—they both longed for a regulated existence. Philippe Lambert and Laurence Duclos married a year later and moved into an apartment in Rue Dorian near Place de la Nation, where tall linden trees filtered the sunlight that shone in through the windows. In June 1983 Nicolas was born.

⌇

IT WOULD NOT HAVE come as a surprise if the birth of his child had stoked the smoldering mountain of fear inside Philippe. Every district nurse knows that young parents suffer from an aftershock of anxiety and responsibility a few days after the umbilical cord has been cut. Even those without a nervous disposition. There, in the cot or on the breast or lying between them, is their Achilles' heel. Nobody warned them about this sudden vulnerability and if someone did mention it, they weren't listening.

But while Laurence wondered out loud how she could carry on living if anything ever happened to this tiny human being, Philippe became the picture of serenity. He changed diapers, fed the baby (breastfeeding was not a success and they soon switched to formula), and was deeply content to break with French custom by exhausting his supply of free days to spend the first weeks fathering his son. "Nothing will ever happen to him," he told Laurence. "He will always stay healthy, grow very old, and never break so much as a finger. Believe me."

Those first summery weeks, Nicolas cried only when the twilight was starting to fade. Every evening around ten, Philippe let his exhausted wife fall asleep on the couch, took his son in his arms, and carried him all the way around Place de la Nation, following the sidewalk of the outermost ring, where the child's howls invariably calmed. Back in the apartment, he stroked the baby's gently pulsing head, laid him over his shoulder, and continued to walk to and fro in the kitchen until the tense little body relaxed against the side of his neck. Fear had never been further away.

THAT SOMEONE WOULD COME to look after the child was a given. Philippe and his brothers and sister had grown up with these temporary, caring, shadowy figures around the house. Young women whose names and builds changed, but whose hands and voices melted together in the children's memories to a single movement, a single feeling. Hands that dressed you, made meals, packed bags, pushed baby carriages, retrieved balls from flower beds, tidied and picked things up, checked the temperature of the bathwater, and combed wet hair. Silhouettes that appeared in the morning, waved goodbye, stood waiting at the school gates, never sitting down but always sliding between the salon and the playroom, the kitchen and the bathroom. Disappearing at a certain moment to their *chambre de bonne* on the top floor by slipping out the back door, through which they made their equally silent entrance again the next day. Until the end of Philippe's *collège*, their presence was self-evident. He couldn't imagine it being any different for his children; Laurence soon came round. Nicolas was an easy child, Philippe seemed more balanced than ever in the time she had known him, she missed work, and her parents-in-law were willing not only to search for a girl for them but also pay and house her; the maid's room on the eighth floor at Rue Marbeau was empty, after all. Times had changed: An international au pair seemed a good, modern variant of the classic nanny.

"I'll look in the northern countries," Ghislaine said. "I don't want my grandson adopting an African accent or starting to use Arabic words. What's more, girls from the north are clean and quick to learn the language. We'll look for a new one each year, that's how it's done these days." After having worried most about her youngest son, she was happy to be able to contribute to his perfect, mail-order family.

"Let me take care of it. That's best for everyone."

⌒

LATER, WHEN PHILIPPE THINKS back on these years, the first three with Nicolas, they seem a bright, timeless intermezzo. The

days thread together in calm happiness. He goes to work and occu-
pies himself with pleasant, abstract activities: He's responsible for
cost minimization. Planning a new production line, relocating
jobs, mainly to Asia—these are all major developments involving
thousands of employees, packaged as numbers and pastel-colored
histograms on overheads he explains at weekly meetings.

In the evening, he returns to a neat, fresh-smelling apartment,
where his son has been bathed and fed. Philippe says, "See you
tomorrow," to the au pair who lives on the other side of town in a
maid's room above his parental home, pleasantly out of sight. He
waits for Laurence, they warm up something from Picard Surgelés
in the microwave, drink a glass of wine. He makes love to his wife at
least twice a week. She has recovered her shy prenatal enthusiasm
and likes to walk around the house naked, which excites him.
Sometimes they smoke a joint—buying Dutch weed from the cook
at the brasserie around the corner and airing the bedroom afterward.

Within a few months of becoming a parent, Philippe no longer
remembers what he was like before. He forgets the constant tension
in his neck, the headaches, the nights he only skimmed the surface
of sleep, he forgets the calamitous visions that beset him through
his entire childhood and adolescence, flaring up at any moment.
Visions he has never mentioned to anyone, that not even Laurence
knows about: dead animals on the side of the road, torn-off limbs,
a body floating in the river, water washing away houses, a child
choking on candy, an unending stream of cockroaches from under
the baseboards, toppling bookcases crushing toddlers, chain colli-
sions, diseases that make your tongue turn black. He forgets that
those images were always there. He forgets what fear feels like.
This phase of his life is so bright, almost bleached, a sun-drenched
impression. For the first time in his thirty years of being alive he
approaches the future trustingly, without reservations, and slowly
that starts to feel normal. Philippe starts to believe that it will continue like this forever.

THIS ISN'T NECESSARILY STRANGE. Fears can grow, but they can also shrink, disappearing as inexplicably as they appeared. But around Philippe, outside the brightly lit cage of his happiness, the city is moving in the opposite direction.

In mid-July 1983 a bomb explodes at the Turkish Airlines check-in desk at Orly Airport. Eight dead, fifty wounded; the atrocity is claimed by the Syrian branch of the Armenian liberation army ASALA—almost no one understands how these things could possibly be linked. "Paris in Fear," declares the cover of *Time* magazine. Air traffic comes to a brief standstill (not for too long, it's the summer holidays, the middle of the exodus of Parisians fleeing the hot city) and more police appear in the Metro corridors. But it is remarkable how quickly the attack is rationalized away. This is an attack on Turkey, not France. On French territory, true, but . . . This hatred is directed elsewhere. Laurence too, still at home on maternity leave when it happens, simply heads off to the airport to start work again at the end of the summer. Philippe looks at his son, confident that they are invulnerable behind his shield of foolish bliss. The months pass quietly. Nicolas gets his first teeth, crawls, stands up on his chubby legs and takes his first steps in the presence of the au pair, who has him repeat the trick later in front of his parents. He grows, he starts talking—there has never been a brighter or more beautiful child in all of France.

NOBODY KNOWS WHEN FROGS realize that the water is about to boil. Nobody decides where the tipping point is going to be; such critical moments can only be identified in hindsight. Just before Christmas 1983, a bomb explodes in the ventilation system of three-star restaurant Le Grand Véfour in the Palais Royal. The ten wounded are riddled with glass, crystal, and porcelain from the windows, chandeliers, plates, and bowls. There are no fatalities, no suspects are identified.

There is an attack on a Marks & Spencer department store in February 1985 and, a month later, another on the Rivoli Beaubourg cinema, actions people interpret as targeting a Zionist chairman and a Jewish film festival. "It's terrible," they say over aperitifs and office coffees. "Antisemitism is still among us." For many Parisians, that "us" feels very distant, even if that's something they don't say out loud. On Minitel, which delivers the news to their homes faster than newspapers ever could, events are reduced to white block letters on a black screen. People are scared, but not scared enough. That comes later.

MAYBE IT'S BECAUSE OF the pictures, produced more quickly with each attack, sometimes already being printed in color. Maybe it's because of the reporters, arriving at the scene faster and faster and now specially trained in how to cover events like these. They have learned not to approach those in charge first, but to get their quotes from: one—victims who are still capable of providing a response; two—the most distraught eyewitnesses; three—the emergency services, preferably in action with bandages and bags of blood.

Maybe somebody finally articulates the right word, a word so precise and powerful that it gnaws its way deep into the populace, making people quicken their pace on the street and anchoring fear in their consciousness—a fear that can no longer be expelled by sleep. But whatever the process, in the course of 1985, the acts and attacks become "a wave." The incidents are no longer isolated.

On December 7, 1985—the city is getting ready for Christmas—bombs explode among the shoppers in Galeries Lafayette and Printemps Haussmann. More than forty casualties lie between the shattered china services in the basement of one department store and in the perfume section of the other. One of the first reporters calls it a "hellish odorama": perfume mixed with the smells of blood, urine, and sweat. The TV keeps replaying footage of collapsed Christmas decorations, shocked shoppers, blood-smeared marble floors, and scattered shopping bags.

"Lafayette and Printemps" comes to be seen as that tipping point. It can now happen anywhere, it can happen to anyone, you can't arm yourself against chaos unless it's by giving up your public life, and that would mean "giving up our French soul," as the mayor of Paris, Jacques Chirac, puts it. The government urges everyone to be alert for abandoned luggage, to notify the authorities of suspicious packages, to watch out for "conspicuous behavior," even if nobody knows exactly what that means. From out of nowhere, *Hezbollah* has become a household word, forcing its way into daily conversation.

February 1986 is a chain of black days. In the month people traditionally prefer to skip on their way to spring, a bomb explodes at a hotel on the Champs-Élysées, an explosive device on the third floor of the Eiffel Tower is dismantled at the last minute, packages explode in Gibert Jeune and FNAC bookstores. The targets are vague and that's what's most frightening. Look, they say, there's no longer any doubt, French life itself has been taken hostage. Our culture, our music, our way of life.

There is an explosion on a high-speed train from Paris to Lyon, taking the number of injured up to eighty-seven. Spring is as bleak and pale as the face of President Mitterrand, who can't find the words to reassure the nation. On March 20, the sense of shock amplifies again because there are fatalities again—that's how quickly people have adjusted; as long as there are only injuries, it's not too bad. Nobody remembers amputated legs or ruptured eyes. Nobody remembers the woman who has lost the ability to speak or the man who will be haunted by this moment for the rest of his life.

A bomb explodes at the entrance of the shopping arcade Galerie Point Show on the Champs-Élysées. After hearing the muffled bang, the audience in the adjoining cinema flee outside and find a horror movie on the sidewalk. "All the shop windows, all that glass, all that blood," a young man stammers into a camera. His gaping eyes, the numb faces around him, the flashing lights, the blood, the newspaper headlines (c'est la guerre!) become the ingredients for extra news bulletins that already seem familiar.

To Philippe the news feels like reports from another country. He switches the TV off with the remote control and takes his son to Jardin de Reuilly, a new park in the neighborhood. Because of the terrorism, the trash cans have been removed and replaced with jerry-rigged contraptions, transparent green plastic bags hanging from rings in the spring breeze. They've been set up all over the city, in the Metro, on the Champs-Élysées, where Japanese tourists take photos of them. He brushes off Laurence's warnings. ("Be careful on public transport, take the car instead, if it gets busy you have to leave, Philippe, do you hear me?") With his son on his shoulders, he is inviolable. He is looking forward to the summer holiday at Cap d'Antibes, he is looking forward to announcing his imminent promotion during Sunday dinner at his parents', he is looking forward to every single day.

⁓

SHE'S SEVENTEEN. A LITTLE young, but Ghislaine is impressed by her application's impeccable French and her bonbon of a name: Eloïse Schiller. Besides working full-time in her parents' hotel in Tübingen, she has also completed her Gymnasium Abitur and would like to spend a year as an au pair in Paris before studying international relations. "I adore children and have a ten-year-old brother and a six-year-old sister whom I love very much." The passport photo shows an apple-shaped face crowned by two thick, reddish-blond braids. No makeup.

She would like to come a little earlier, on July 1, 1986, to get used to the city. That's convenient because their current au pair, the third one, has been homesick all year. Dutch Chantal, from a town with the tongue-twisting name of 's-Gravenzande, doesn't need a single second to think about whether she'd like to stop a couple of weeks early—her suitcase is already packed and waiting.

AS AGREED, LAURENCE SPENDS half a day explaining Eloïse's duties and letting her meet Nicolas before Philippe arrives home. "The contact with the father of the family can be difficult at first for a young au pair. Build this up gradually." It's their first years as employers and they do everything according to the tips provided by the agency Ghislaine has engaged. When Philippe comes home on Tuesday, July 1, 1986, the full-figured girl in tight jeans is standing on the play rug. She turns toward him and says, while curtseying, "Eloïse." Philippe sees ginger lashes above greenish eyes that are looking up at him, below them an accumulation of round shapes—then he doesn't see anything at all. He's collapsed in the hall of their apartment.

WHEN HE COMES TO, the shocked au pair has already left for her *chambre de bonne.* "Thank God," is his first thought. Thank God she's gone. In the living room where he's been laid on the couch, an ambulance driver is talking calmly to Laurence. Blood pressure normal, heart rate normal, brain activity normal, everything is normal, madame, we can only wait until your husband regains consciousness. Take it easy, monsieur, just stay there. You're at home in your own apartment. Nothing to worry about, everything will be fine.

Reassuring murmurs, the sound of documents being filled in, the light of lamps they've turned on, although it's nowhere near nighttime—Philippe follows it all as through a layer of foam. Readings are taken, lights are shone into his eyes—try and sit up now, calmly, on a straight chair—reflexes, a mouthful of water, the cuff around his arm once again.

After the paramedic has left, he can't explain what happened. Maybe he didn't have enough to eat today, a busy day, the heat that has settled over the city? He's exhausted, goes to bed, and leaves for the Renault head office in Boulogne-Billancourt the following morning as usual. There he spends a long time staring out through the windows that take up almost the entire wall. From his sixth-floor office he has a view of the Seine, which curls around this neighborhood like a lasso. In the course of the day the hazy July sky fills with smog. Planes draw their patterns to and from Orly, traffic flows along the avenue like a second river—a familiar spectacle unfolding on the other side of the double glazing, accompanied by the soundtrack of work. The rustle of air-conditioning, the constant ringing of the telephone in his secretary's adjoining office, the krrtkkkrrrt-kkkkrrrrt of the fax, all noises that should reassure him. But he feels his left eye drooping. He skips the lunch outside, unable to bear the thought of the busy brasserie, the steak tartare, the salad, the wine, and the heavy feeling that slows the pace of work for a couple of hours afterward.

On the deserted floor, the realization of what he already knew just before he passed out sinks in: It's back. The fear. Like a patient dog that sits outside the supermarket waiting for its master even if he takes three years to do the shopping. An old, troublesome, abandoned dog that now stands up, wagging its tail, ready to once again stick by his side, a step behind or a step ahead, but never far away.

IT'S ELOÏSE.

It can't be anything else; the fear struck the instant he laid eyes on her. Eloïse, a girl so innocent he initially rejected the idea that the two things could be related. Eloïse, who timidly awaits him the next day and asks in a frightened voice if "it's going all right now, monsieur." She turns eighteen in September, a child still. Philippe wonders what possessed her parents to let her go to Paris by herself. Eloïse is irrefutably good with children, at least. After just three days, shy little Nicolas automatically holds out his hand when they're going out together and calls her "Ooweetha" with his childish lisp. They play peekaboo, she sings him to sleep in lilting Southern German and has him eating all kinds of food—Laurence is so enthusiastic about her new au pair that she's already forgotten that Philippe fainted the first time he saw her. It's simply inconceivable that the two things could be connected.

But Philippe notices that his stomach shrinks in Eloïse's presence, that he has trouble breathing and gets a stabbing pain in his left shoulder. He doesn't like to look at her; he avoids being in the same room and does his utmost to keep the period after he's come home, when the au pair is still busy tidying up the last bit of mess or rounding off Nicolas's bath-time ritual, as brief as possible. Any excuse to send the girl home an hour earlier. She doesn't object but disappears to the Metro, to her room, offstage.

At night it's not the old images that pursue him. These are much less clear, more colors than shapes, more smells than images: smells that are still so strong in his nose when he wakes up in a cold sweat in the middle of the night that he tries to wash them out after he's given in and gone into the bathroom for a while. He stares at his sleeping son's face, dimly lit by a Care Bears night-light. He stares at Laurence's face in the glow from the streetlight shining in through the chink in the curtains. She is relaxed, the hair that is so like a helmet in the daytime loose on the pillow, her bare and narrow shoulders defenseless. He touches her gently. She doesn't wake. There is no reason to be afraid. Before, there was always a reason, a specific threat, a concrete suspicion of disaster that would strike in his vicinity. Now he doesn't have a clue about the cause or purpose of his fear. He goes back to bed, climbing between sheets that are still clammy from his sweat a half hour earlier. He falls asleep anyway and it starts all over again: doors that refuse to open, facades that go on forever, a road that suddenly cracks open, and a murky, stinking sky. Above all this, he sometimes sees a pale green haze; on awakening he pushes away the thought that it's the color of Eloïse's eyes.

When he leaves for the office at eight, he feels like a fifty-year-old.

EVENTUALLY, LAURENCE STARTS WORRYING. "Maybe you went back to work too soon," she says, tossing the newspaper onto the breakfast table. It's been quiet for a few months, but now there's been a new attack on police headquarters: one dead, thirty wounded. "Or maybe the attacks are getting to you, they're bothering me too. I'm going to ask your parents if we can come down south a little earlier. A couple of weeks' vacation would do you good, you're always so relaxed there." Yes, maybe she's right. Philippe doesn't under any circumstances want to tell her what's going on; he's always carefully concealed his problems from her and in the end they've always resolved themselves. Fears can disappear the way they came, he remembers that and clings to it now. It has to stop. This has to stop.

WHILE THEY'RE WAITING TO check in at Orly, Eloïse strolls into view. For a moment Philippe, startled, thinks that she's come to see them off. Bizarre. But she has a case with her.

"Oh, honey, I told you that, didn't I? Did I forget?" Laurence looks up at him, she doesn't see the problem. "I was able to get an extra ticket. I thought it would actually give us some peace and quiet and"—the child is now standing before them—"otherwise she'd just be by herself in Paris, and this way Eloïse will see a bit of the country too, Eloïse, *n'est-ce pas?*" Nicolas is jumping up and down at the end of her arm, shouting, "Ooweetha, Ooweetha," then grabs hold of Eloïse's round calves. She's decked herself in a floral jersey frock for the trip.

It's like we've got a teenage daughter with us, thinks Philippe, beads of sweat forming on his upper lip. One who doesn't realize that breasts like that really stretch such a tight top, T-shirt, thing, whatever it is. The women he's usually around aren't like that, the women at the office hide their anorexic forms in two-piece business ensembles with padded shoulders and a tight belt around the waist, Thierry Mugler–style. His own wife only had curves when she was pregnant; Laurence is more a *garçonne*, all the women he knows are. He is ashamed of the embarrassment he feels at boarding with this creamy, curvy, oh-so-German girl, and that's not all: The pain in his left shoulder is back. On the plane he swaps seats with her, so "she can be closer to Nicolas." Even before lunch he's asked the stewardess for a glass of wine. "You know what, make it a cognac."

⁓

NORMALLY PHILIPPE ADAPTS TO the life they lead during their annual vacation on Cap d'Antibes as if slipping between the pages of a family photo album. The peninsula, with its languid history of spas, polo games, old money, and casinos, is the luminous positive to exhausted *fin-de-saison* Paris, where the population is dragging itself to the finish line. He generally leaves the city behind the moment the plane takes off.

The Lamberts have hardly any luggage, the badge of the privileged. A complete, light-colored wardrobe that hasn't changed for years is waiting at the house for each family member, and for Laurence too, since her admission to their circle. Some articles of clothing have lasted twenty years: wide, loose pants and linen shirts and halter dresses that have remained immune to all fashion trends. After a few days, the family members are so tanned that everyone looks attractive. Father and now grandfather Lambert, retired chairman of La Poste, only appears in baggy, rib jersey T-shirts, cargo pants, and espadrilles. Ghislaine walks barefoot around the house in sun-bleached Elizabeth Taylor caftans, her dyed hair protected by a turban. Sometimes Justine comes for a week with her twins; her husband always stays in the city to continue working. The two elder brothers appear now and then with their families, preferably not at the same time. Philippe always stays for the whole month of August; Laurence tries to arrange her work around it too. Everyone immediately relaxes into this world of down-at-heel and therefore even more distinguished luxury. Not bought but inherited—family luxury. The first time she joined Philippe's family here, Laurence prepared herself. From her experience as a stewardess she was able to fabricate an acceptable vacation history for herself: trips to Nice, a summer in Germany, driving through Italy. She knew what to say if the conversation required an appropriate anecdote. Now, after four summers on the peninsula, she knows that her concern was unwarranted. No one ever asked her about her background; for the Lamberts she is a woman without a past. Her life began by joining the family. Beyond that there are no lives, at least no lives one needs to become deeply acquainted with. The days glide by in thoughtless dissipation and conversations are no more than a hand trailing through water.

THE HEAT WAVE OF summer 1986 is, like every year's, sudden and scorching. The canicule brings lethargy, the necessity of adopting the tempo of a salamander. The rhythm generally has a beneficial influence on Philippe. In the morning, they usually go diving off Plage des Ondes, a family hobby Philippe likes to watch while snorkeling, floating in the great blue, arms and legs wide. He also loves the hours of inertia after lunch, sitting under the pergola on the north side of the house, where there is no direct sunlight. Remnants of wine in the glasses, picked chicken bones on the plates with stubbed cigarettes between them. The dying conversations and the siesta to a chorus of cicadas that follows; it's all equally reassuring and meaningless. The rest of the afternoon everyone does their own thing, at most a little *bronzage*, sunbathing on the small beach within walking distance of the villa, and otherwise it's the big wait for the cool of evening. This year it should be even more relaxing. Nicolas's toddler rhythm is not yet attuned to the adults', but they have Eloïse to take care of that. After his afternoon nap, already ending by the time the adults have shuffled off to their rooms for a siesta, she plays with him under the pergola. The highest SPF available in the house is 8, little help with her milky skin. She protects herself as well as she can against the sun's onslaught with a large hat, hastily purchased in a tourist shop in Juan-les-Pins, and an old pareu belonging to Philippe's sister. And while Eloïse nonetheless slowly turns an orangey red that first week, Laurence and Philippe could devote themselves to lazy afternoon sex, isolated in a room in the east wing of the terra-cotta villa, out of earshot. In the evenings they could take off to go and drink cocktails, like during their first summer.

Or at least that was how Laurence had imagined it while preparing for these weeks. She is now thirty, Nicolas three. In the ideal picture she has been carefully constructing since meeting Philippe, the gap between the first child and a possible second is getting a little too large. Relaxation and siestas are perfect for conception.

PHILIPPE IS SITTING ON the side of the bed. Laurence drinks a little too much during these lunches and has sunk into her first sleep, on her stomach with her limbs spread. In this empty hour he would love to be able to follow her example and surrender consciousness. He has never found imposed rest during the heat of the day easy, but in the past few years, since Nicolas's birth, his body has seemed to suddenly get it: that it could disappear without sleeping deeply, briefly turning its back on the world to become a formless form, an element without limitations, at one with the slightly trembling air, exactly the right temperature inside and out, with no dividing line between them. What deep relaxation that could bring.

An enviable state, visible in his wife, who experiences it with a soft rustling in her throat, an innocent little snore. The small white triangle her bikini bottom has left on her buttocks shines in the semidarkness. He wishes he was lying next to her, in the same pool of sleep. Soon she will surface from the depths and feel the bed next to her with her tanned hand, searching for him. He wishes he was looking forward to it.

But no. He's been in the summer house for almost two weeks and he still can't relax. Too restless to sleep, too restless to close his eyes and just listen to the cicadas and the thin curtains sliding over the wooden floor in a warm gust of wind. His whole body resists lying down, relaxing, disappearing—he can't manage it. He no longer wants to try, that's why he's now sitting on the side of the bed. His back is stiff. In the filtered light his thighs are like two lifeless logs his hands rest upon. His listless member is inert between them, useless now for some time. He stands up silently, pulls on his shorts and a T-shirt, and pads on the dry, cracked soles of his summer feet through the tiled hall that links the wing to the house.

ELOÏSE IS UNDER THE pergola. Philippe can see her through the bamboo fly curtain. He stays behind it, camouflaged by the darkness of the shuttered living room, inaudible with the strings of hard beads clicking quietly against each other. The girl is only a few feet away, five at most, her broad pink back to the doorway. She has her reddish hair up in a high ponytail, the strands that have escaped are stuck to her sweaty neck. She's hot, of course she is. With her blond constitution, she retains the heat much more than the olive-skinned Lamberts.

The pergola is partly covered with rush mats, partly over-grown by a large wisteria that lets specks of light shine through. Minuscule but sharply defined, the shadows mix with the freckles on Eloïse's upper arms and the side of her face; she's looking away from Philippe. Green glass hearts are dangling from her ears. She never takes them off. While Nicolas pushes small plastic boats through a large tub of water and makes the sputtering noise of an outboard, she bends slightly forward over her postcards. She's bought two varieties: a reproduction of a brightly colored historic poster of a woman diving, caught in midair and watched by two bronzed swimmers—an Art Deco interpretation of the good life on the Med—and a collage of photos of Juan-les-Pins, cut into circles and linked by garish lettering and clumsy floral garlands. Eloïse takes a card from one stack and then the other in turn, flips each one over, and, with swift mechanical strokes, fills the back with round, teenage handwriting, the ballpoint wedged in her tightly clenched fist. She is singing softly, nodding along to an imagined rhythm: "You take my self, you take my self-control," a hit from a couple of years ago. Laura Branigan—Philippe recognizes it.

What could she be writing? Philippe thinks. Nothing ever happens, it's as hot as ever, hopefully you're all well, I'm bored, the little boy is sweet, I miss you, my French is improving—he can only come up with platitudes, as if nothing else could ever flow from her pen. He realizes that he doesn't have the slightest idea what goes on inside the au pair's head and also that he's never wondered if anything does go on inside her or in any of these girls in general.

Philippe has always found that a pleasant aspect of the relation-ship: the not knowing, the not caring either. In a way, their thoughts and emotions are something you shouldn't be interested in, just as there's no need for you to be interested in the precise workings of a washing machine. They have to do their job, prefer-

ably on time and without making too much noise. If you empa-
thized with your staff, it would be impossible to tell them what to
do. Life would have too many ramifications.

Philippe thinks of his university friend Martin, now a diplo-
mat, whose long nose and red eye sockets have always reminded
him of a macaque. Not so long ago they bumped into each other in
the FNAC, patted each other on the shoulder, *mon vieux*, how's
your son, how was Hanoi . . .

"You have to replace the staff every three months," Martin told
him over a quick coffee standing at the bar. "Nannies, gardeners,
the lot. Otherwise you become attached to each other, relationships
form, it gets messy. The last thing you want is having to explain to
the ministry how you got a maid pregnant or the hijinks you got
up to with the chauffeur." There was something monkeyish about
his laugh too: tight lips and too many teeth.

"Sometimes I get their names mixed up, they look so similar,
you know."

"Since Nicolas we've had an au pair," Philippe told him. "The
fourth just started."

"Ah, au pairs . . . that's another thing altogether," Martin said
as he crushed a sugar cube into his café serré. "Lucky you. I don't
have kids, otherwise I'd definitely get one. What am I saying? I'd
get two. Eighteen-year-olds, blond, Swedish . . ." He laughed again,
drumming on the zinc of the bar with his fingertips. "And no
employer to take them away again after three months. Yes, you're a
lucky dog." Philippe laughed along awkwardly. He'd never actually thought about au pairs in those terms and definitely not about
this fresh-faced, redheaded Eloïse, who managed to instill such
restlessness in him all the same.

SHE'S STILL WRITING. Philippe watches. Why does his body tense up
so completely at the sight of this young woman? How is it possible

that he wants to spend every moment of the day close to her and is disgusted by it at the same time? It's not lust, Philippe is sure of that. He doesn't desire her. But at the same time, he feels an almost uncontrollable urge to *overpower* her—ashamed of the word even as he thinks it. Hidden here like this, he finds the courage to admit to himself that it's only with the greatest possible effort that he is able to stop himself from bursting through the bamboo curtain and throwing himself on the ground with Eloïse. Although the idea fills him with distaste, his body is continually driving him toward it: clasping all those curves to him in one embrace, like an ape, arms and legs at once, and pressing down on her with all his weight to restrain her. It's absurd. He thinks about it when she's sitting next to them reading on the beach, when she's in the back of the car with Nicolas on her lap, when she sits down at the end of the table for dinner, when he bumps into her by accident—and God knows how hard he tries to avoid it—in the hall or, even worse, on the stairs. To suddenly leap on that stack of padded excess. That's what he wants. No, it's what he *must*. Rolling down the stairs, her soft flesh gripped tightly by his limbs. That's as far as his imagination goes, it's what has to happen, the scene that plays out in his mind over and over again, taking control of his body.

Philippe gets even hotter than the midday heat around him. Pores dilate, he feels sweat on his scalp, he blushes in the darkness. He reaches for his crotch in an idiotic attempt to check what he already knows—no, not at all, there is nothing about this girl that excites him. He is an embarrassment. His thoughts disgust him. They're not even thoughts, it's a sick propensity, a compulsion that has taken control of him. Is he power-drunk, a feeling he's never had before and doesn't recognize? Is he mentally ill, perverse, a brute disguised as the educated scion of a respectable family? Does he want to get rid of her? Is he, just say it, insane? No, no, no . . . But what, then, if none of that? Can't he just leave her in peace?

Can't they just hide her away again in that German town among the cuckoo clocks and the Alpine meadows or whatever they have there?

Nicolas stops sputtering, scoops the boats out of the tub, and turns his little head. "Papa?" Eloïse stops humming, looks up, and says in her basic French: "Non, Nicolas, papa pas là. Papa dort." Shocked, Philippe is already retreating soundlessly across the cotton rug between the low couches, through the long hall, and into the cool kitchen, where he glugs down a glass of water.

THIS SCENE REPEATS SEVERAL times in the course of the vacation on Cap d'Antibes. Philippe spies on Eloïse beside the swimming pool, under the pergola again, from the passage where she has fled into the shadowy living room to escape the outside heat. Philippe learns to merge into the hall, the wallpaper, a shaded corner of the porch. By nature, he's a man who doesn't make a lot of noise or take up a lot of space, partly a result of being a fourth child, but also a question of character. That's useful now. When he's out of the way, around a corner, watching Eloïse, his breathing is inaudible, his movement as quiet as a cat's. He observes the girl closely, seeing how unsuspectingly she picks her nose, how consistently nice she is to his son, how she never raises her voice. How she, on the odd occasion when Nicolas drifts off to sleep again in the empty hours of the siesta, lays him down on the couch in the living room and sits next to him to read, or falls asleep herself. Once, he sees her making a furtive call on the Lamberts' telephone. Speaking German in subdued tones, she takes her time; it must be a pricey call home to her family, or maybe a boyfriend, what does Philippe know? He stands in the hall and watches her fiddling with the coiled cord, sees her scratch the inside of her thigh, the way she lifts her heavy hair up off her neck. Always the moment comes when he has to rapidly withdraw. He feels dirty, bad, stupid.

A feeling not even a hundred laps of the swimming pool can wash away.

As the end of the vacation approaches, he feels relief—anything is better than this.

Deeply frustrated, Laurence can't wait either.

THEY RETURN TO PARIS on August 31, inserting the key in the lock of their apartment on Rue Dorian at six p.m. They put down their bags and carry the sleeping Nicolas through to his bedroom, putting him to bed, clothes and all. The apartment has been closed for the entire hot month and smells of warm furniture. Laurence raises the shutters and opens the windows in the living room and their bedroom. Philippe gets a bottle of white burgundy out of the fridge, which they left on, and thinks: Just like this fridge, I can simply skip this summer and carry on from where we left off. Cap d'Antibes is there; this is here, this is home. There's Laurence on the couch, my wife, with such a fantastic tan. It's strange how we never notice how much more attractive the sun has made us until we're back in the city. My son is in bed, we have the evening to ourselves. I'll tell her that in a minute. I feel like undressing her. Maybe next year we'll go somewhere else, a whole month of Lamberts might be a bit too much. I feel like peeling down her skirt, making love to her on the couch, or on the floor, with the windows wide open, while darkness falls. Tomorrow we'll go back to work, the girl will appear here again, and then I can simply forget the way I've acted these last few weeks, nullifying it. It was a mistake. Heat-induced foolishness, strange behavior I won't need to explain if I just leave it there. It was nothing, it is nothing. Tomorrow I'll sit at my desk and resume work where I left off. In a clean shirt that will make my tanned hands look even darker, I will carry on with the file Carrosseries Merging/Outsourcing.

Laurence is sitting on the couch, sticky from the trip, and she too decides to forget the vacation. Dwelling on setbacks never helped her get ahead. Inside her there is a hard essence that demands progress and has always saved her. A second child, a second car, a promotion to purser, in a few years, a new apartment, those are things you can work on. Focus. Philippe will get back to his old self, he'll come round, he has to, her plan demands it and a slight hiccup doesn't make any difference. She turns toward him, smiles with the tip of her tongue visible between her teeth. All things considered, he's already looking a lot more attractive. She accepts the wine and they clink bedewed glasses.

⁓

A COUPLE OF DAYS later, during the evening rush hour, a loud bang sounds at the nearby Gare de Lyon. On an RER train that is just filling with commuters, a bag starts smoldering. A young woman with "Like a Virgin"–style hair jumps up and screams. Her pet hamster panics and leaps out of the inside pocket of her leather jacket, into the crowded compartment. The detonator that caused the bang is connected to thirteen explosive charges, but the wiring was faulty. If it had gone off the package would have been sure to devastate the entire car and derail the train if it had already left the station; the passengers have escaped a bloodbath. The hamster is later found squashed next to the bag of armed explosives. A marine in a bomb suit carries the tiny corpse along the platform on his glove.

THE PARISIANS ARE BACK. Back in their city and back to the violence. They thought they could forget it on the beaches of the Mediterranean and in the French Alps and with family in Auvergne, but that was a delusion. In September 1986 it's like the sirens never fall silent. The city's residents live day and night with alarms swelling, disappearing into the distance, or ascending the tall facades that line their streets. The fire department, police, ambulances, usually in that order. One attack has hardly been committed, called in, traced, triaged, assessed, treated, cleared, reported, typed out, recorded, broadcast, commentated on, and mourned before the next has taken place. The fire department is continually turning out for false alarms; suspicious packages are everywhere.

On September 8, just before closing time, a bomb explodes in the post office of the Hôtel de Ville. A fifty-one-year-old employee, Marguerite Thuault, dies on the spot. Her unsuspecting husband and twenty-year-old son are watching television when her name is announced on the news. Among the eighteen wounded is a three-year-old girl—it's always the details that stick with you, the things frowning people tell each other in subdued voices: "Imagine being that son . . . and a girl of three, have things got so bad that a girl of three . . ." It's no longer just the headlines. Jacques Chirac, now prime minister, has also taken to using the word *war*.

These words resonate four days later, on September 12, when forty-one people are wounded at the other end of the city's central axis, in the new business district of La Défense. Until now a distant and fairly abstract construction site, at one stroke it is seen as part of the heart of the city; nothing unites like suffering. Here too, yes, even here, maybe especially here, in the city's most recent extension, life in freedom is under fire.

The numbers of lightly and badly wounded are still being established when attention returns to the center of town two days later, on September 14. A waitress spots a bag that has been left in Pub Renault on the Champs-Élysées. Her boss and three security guards successfully remove it from the crowded restaurant, a complex of walkways and mezzanines above the car manufacturer's showroom. The instructions the authorities have been pounding into the population for a few years now are followed to a T. Pricking their salads, smearing foie gras on perfectly crispy squares of toast, and looking out through the enormous windows at the tourists strolling along the famous avenue, the guests are oblivious. A moment later in the parking garage the bomb goes off after all, blasting a deep crater in the concrete floor. One of the security guards doesn't survive the explosion.

A couple of hours later the prime minister appears on TV to announce that all non-Europeans wishing to enter France will require a visa and that the army will be carrying out the customs checks. "Is that what you do in a war?" grumbles a farmer in Périgord as he turns off the small TV in his kitchen. "Ask for a visa? They're mad. Tomorrow it'll happen again, mark my word." And he's proven right. The next day, a rainy Monday, September 15, less than twenty-four hours later, a man in a gray raincoat walks into police headquarters on the Île de la Cité and heads for the office that issues driver's licenses. It's one of the few public areas in the enormous building and it's busy. Since the attack on the police in July, security has been heightened—but still. The bomb remains unnoticed under the man's large coat; he's able to leave it under a chair. People and furniture are blown apart. The windows along the service counters shatter, sheets of modular ceiling collapse. With one dead and fifty-five wounded, it is the bloodiest attack in the series. Doctors and nurses with stretchers come running out of the Hôtel-Dieu on the other side of the road and ambulances are dispatched from other hospitals in the surrounding area. The day ends with sirens, flashing lights, and more sirens, all muffled by the humid air.

THE RENTRÉE, THE NEW season, is only two weeks old and already there are three dead and 116 wounded. Calls go up to close the schools, to bring public life to a standstill. Hotel bookings are canceled, the Metro is less busy. Half-empty buses do their circuits of the boulevards, an image of impotence.

Since their return from Cap d'Antibes, Philippe and Laurence have been trying to lead a normal life. Planes take off from Orly as usual, the factories are still turning out cars, their work has resumed. Laurence borrows her mother-in-law's car, which would otherwise be sitting motionless at Rue Marbeau, so that she and Philippe can both avoid public transport. The attack at Pub Renault is discussed extensively at the company, of course, but Philippe tries to avoid the lamentations around the conference table. He has a lot of outside appointments, he says.

Eloïse's having to take the Metro to their place every morning and then travel back to her servant's room on the other side of the city in the evening doesn't seem to cause them any particular concern. She has started her French lessons; every day she travels to her course in an annex at the Sorbonne and then from there to their apartment to work. She appears on time and when she leaves again, she disappears into a system that is not part of the Lamberts' life. When Laurence's sister asks her about it during their weekly telephone conversation, Laurence gets tetchy. You have to stay a bit levelheaded, otherwise they're getting what they want, and what's more, our au pair mainly takes line 1, straight from Porte Maillot to Nation. Yes, it *is* the most central line, right through the city from west to east and along the Champs-Élysées, but it's also the line with the highest security, have you seen all the patrols in the city since the summer? No-no-no, it's all going fine. Eloïse is young but she's a sensible girl, she's not going to take any risks.

Laurence is busy enough ignoring the news, getting back into the swing of things without too much fuss, and calming Nicolas, who's been upset since having to start preschool. She's smoking a little more, perhaps. When Eloïse arrives, Laurence goes through the day with her, puts on her uniform, gets into Ghislaine's car, and drives to Orly with the windows open. The half hour in the car is her rite of passage. By the time she's flicked her third Dunhill out of the side window, driven into the parking garage, and climbed out of the car, she is transformed into the stewardess who will look after her business-class passengers to Frankfurt or London and back, smiling, calm, just the way she learned during training.

AFTER THEIR NEW START back in Paris, Philippe sticks it out for four days. Four days of convincing himself the summer madness was a mirage, at most a fading embarrassment. When he arrives home after his first day at work, he greets Eloïse as if she were a stranger; there is nothing to remind him or her that they have just spent weeks dressed in flimsy garments and walking around a boiling hot house in close proximity to each other, let alone that he spied on her at length on multiple occasions. He can forget it, nobody noticed, it might as well have never happened.

But on the Friday after the attack on the commuter train, Philippe decides to leave work in the middle of the day. An irrepressible urge drives him from the office. He tells his colleagues that he is going for lunch with a colleague from the Asia division, picks his car up from the Renault headquarters parking garage, and drives straight to Nation, where he parks a couple of streets away from Rue Dorian. He walks to his own home and takes up position a block away from the apartment building to observe the entrance, the door he goes in and out of every day, passing under trees that have grown imperceptibly thicker and higher over the past few years.

He sees it all as if for the first time. A warm September wind rustles the linden trees, the patches of light caress the tall stucco facades of his building and the identical apartment building next to it. They are set off a little from the street in a small garden, on a piece of land where the original nineteenth-century block was broken open. Across the street it's still all art nouveau doors and massive balconies with decorative wrought iron railings. And then these modernist buildings plonked down in the middle of it all—there's something stodgy and methodical about it, something coarse, the way Philippe imagines East Berlin, if the surroundings weren't so elegant. He has never paid any attention to it before. When they bought the place, he and Laurence mainly looked at the layout of the apartment, the possibilities for a nursery, proximity to public transport, the basement parking. Now he stares at the steel gate he has pushed open so often and imagines the click and the buzz, the quiet clang as it closes. He pictures himself walking around the block, following along behind as he enters the complex through the front door, in and out, in and out, you could set the clock by it. . . .

Eloïse appears. In the street across from his building, Philippe takes a step back. Just as he thought, she's going to pick up Nicolas from preschool. She is wearing sandals and a blue jersey frock, something T-shirt-like again; the girl really has no taste. Her reddish braid stands out brightly against the blue background and is swinging like a pendulum above her large butt. Outside the gate, she turns right. For such a hot day, she is setting a good pace. Philippe is glad the rustling of the trees covers his hasty steps. He should have put on different shoes, not these hard leather soles. He has to do his best to stay within a hundred feet or so, though it helps that he knows where she's going. His heart beats against his rib cage like an angry fist.

Eloïse turns left, straight, right, the preschool is ten minutes' walk from home. Her sturdy calves take turns to gleam in the light, her upper arms, pink as the back of her legs, are tense in her blue dress. She walks like a nurse, Philippe thinks. Do they all walk like that in Germany, perhaps, marching? There's not a grain of elegance in the girl and yet there is something attractive about her robust determination, something that grips him. Here we go again. Philippe clenches his teeth as he makes sure to keep his distance; he doesn't understand what he's doing here. A little later he sees her joining the back of a row of mothers and au pairs to wait for his son. Despite her being so short, she is very present, her hair catching the light among the heads of dark hair.

Philippe waits a good distance away, running the risk of being taken for a pervert. Man, thirtysomething, lingering outside a preschool. The moment Nicolas steps outside in his white shirt and yellow shorts, his round face pale from an exciting morning, Philippe feels his heart rate slow to normal. Calm washes over him like a cool breeze, suddenly there is no longer any necessity to be there. Eloïse has fulfilled her task, she is on time, his child is in good hands. That wasn't the reason for his pursuit anyway; there is no possible explanation for his behavior, none at all.

Knowing that his son has an infallible antenna for the presence of his parents and an owlish ability to rotate his little head 180 degrees on his shoulders, it is now crucial for him to quickly disappear out of Nicolas's field of vision. Philippe takes a different route, coming around behind the two of them again and following at a distance for a few more minutes. Eloïse is carrying the boy's bag, no longer in a hurry; Nicolas is holding her hand and, from the way he is looking up at her, Philippe can see they are talking. He stops on the sidewalk and watches the blue dress and the yellow shorts moving away. Back to his home, the apartment where he shouldn't be at this time of day. He lets them go with a sense of loss, pops into a boulangerie he doesn't usually patronize, and buys an almond croissant he stuffs into his mouth while hurrying back to his car. "The lunch," he tells his secretary half an hour later, "was mediocre."

WHEN HE ARRIVES HOME again, Eloïse seems like a duplicate, not the same person he saw that afternoon. Maybe none of it, once again, was real. Perhaps he hadn't been there at all and just imagined it. The girl leaves for her room and her weekend, out of his system.

The attacks of the following week, on September 8 and 12, are like a rumbling in the distance. He notes that they have taken place and tries to avoid discussing them with Laurence, leaving the panic-mongering to her and her sister, who have begun calling each other more often.

He does develop a new routine. After leaving home in the morning, he first drives to the house of his birth in Rue Marbeau, to wait there on the corner until Eloïse steps out through the front door. She generally takes the Metro in the direction of Porte de la Villette; he follows her at a distance through the streets until he sees her light-colored hair disappearing into the Metro. Then his agitation fades and he hurries back to his car with a soiled feeling. At work he tells them that he is now driving his wife to work first—because of the threat, you know. On Thursday he is almost caught by his own mother, who leaves home at an unusual hour and starts walking directly toward him—fortunately blinded by the morning sun shining down the street. He races around the block, emerges sweatily in the street where he expects Eloïse, and sees her walking ahead of him in the distance.

THE ATTACKS INCREASE AT a frightening rate. On Friday La Défense, on Sunday Pub Renault, on Monday police headquarters. There are no longer any other topics of conversation, radio and TV talk about almost nothing else, even the eyes of the outside world turn to France in shock.

"Starting Wednesday, I'm staying home," Laurence says on Monday evening. "Quite a lot of flights have been canceled, they've merged crews. I'm not really needed." Standing in the kitchen, she turns her back to the sink and looks at Philippe. He seems pale. Less than two weeks back from vacation and it's as if the city air has scoured off his tan. Their first relaxed evening home after the vacation, the tender sex on the couch and the rug, her relief; it's all become a vague recollection. "Last week a friend of Claire's was near the post office when it happened," she says. "She came this close to being killed. And Jean-Luc, you know the one, he had to pick up his new driver's license this week. Just imagine . . ."

"Nonsense," says Philippe. "That's exactly what the terrorists are after, everyone thinking it's just around the corner, that it could happen to anyone, that—"

"Don't be so rational." Laurence slams down her glass. "People have been killed, remember, and a three-year-old girl was wounded. And a friend of my sister's was almost—"

"Almost, yes. Almost." Philippe's voice sounds too high. "The chance of us getting caught up in something like that is nil, zero. It's horrible, but in such a big city, with so many people, the chance is still—"

"You're cold," Laurence says. She gulps down her wine and straightens her bangs. "Or scared. Either way, tomorrow I'm telling Eloïse she doesn't need to come in for the rest of the week and I'm keeping Nicolas home."

That night, an hour after they've fallen asleep with their backs to each other, Philippe wakes up again and spends a long time standing at an open window in the living room. He is not able to tell Laurence that he's scared. So scared, so terribly scared. With a painful, nauseating, head-splitting fear that turns his stomach and weighs down his legs. It's only now he's admitting it to himself. This fear is not about her, it's not for their son. It's focused on the young au pair and that's what makes it impossible to talk about. And he can no longer resist, he can't search for the cause and he doesn't want to; all he can do is give in to it. He has to admit, here and now, that danger is closing in on the girl he has accepted as his responsibility. He perceives it as an enormous, amorphous shadow, sometimes as a rustling that surrounds her. It's the fear of this shadow that drives him and ensures that he, to conquer this fear, must follow that shadow and listen to that rustling. Letting go of all resistance. No longer rationalizing it away like he tried to this evening, not taking practical measures like his wife now, but surrendering to it. From his teenage years he knows that shared fears are met with disbelief. They write you off as mad, cuckoo. Poor boy, we'll look for a treatment, things like that don't occur in our family, your brothers aren't like that at all, we'll hide it away, there's a therapist, you'll grow out of it, stand up straight, that's not us, it's best we don't talk about it anymore—but he doesn't want to talk about it. He can't. He has to listen, there's no other option, he has to listen to it. He can't change the course of what's about to happen, time is rippling like a sheet of fabric that's being gathered in together, all he can do is listen *to prevent the worst*.

⁓

ON THE MORNING OF Wednesday, September 17, 1986, Eloïse Schiller wakes up in her servant's room in Rue Marbeau. It's the sixth gray day in a row; September is making short work of summer. She stays in bed for a while, having no reason to hurry. On Wednesdays she doesn't have lessons and Laurence has unexpectedly told her that she doesn't need to come in for the rest of the week, a few welcome days off after the vacation that wasn't. They can't fool her—in the south she was just a twenty-four-hour babysitter, stuck in a fancy summer house with a randy grandfather commenting on her curves, so *voluptueuse*, a real Rubens. . . . She might only be seventeen, almost eighteen, but she's not stupid. Stuck with that father too, Philippe, who makes her nervous. He's not particularly unfriendly, not especially friendly either, definitely not as horny as the grandpa, but that constant staring is driving her up the wall. And he has such a weird eye, you're never sure he's not looking at you on the sly.

A day off. She crosses her arms behind her head and sings along to the Nordmende transistor radio her father gave her as a going-away present. Her father, who calls her chubby cheeks, my little dumpling, *meine kleine Kugel*—oh, so many reasons to be glad she's here, far from home. Far from the hotel and the guests, the dirty carpets in the corridors, the spattered sinks, the grimy sheets, the hair (hair!) everywhere. Everything that always needs cleaning, that always gets dirty again and then needs cleaning again . . . Away from the beds she has to make with hospital corners, sheets that are never tight enough, sore fingers from all that pulling and tugging. Away from those two little brats; thinking of her little brother and sister now she even feels a slight, sharp, pleasant pang of missing them. Away from the never-ending chores, setting the tables for breakfast, serving mugs of beer to guests with fingers like sausages, always the guests, guests from early in the morning to late at night. It was like living on a stage, other people's eyes all the time. . . . And something else, she's always known that Tübingen wasn't her final destination, just somewhere she was passing through, a gate to something greater. Paris is a good start, but not her first choice. London would have been better, but this was the possibility that presented itself. And if she gets on top of this, she can do anything. *Ahhh baby, my heart is full of love and desire for you / so come on down and do what you've got to do* . . . The Communards on the radio, she loves the video for this song. At the family's, in the daytime, she often turns on *Music Box* and sometimes they play it. She doesn't sing along with the shrieking lead singer but with the female singer with the low voice, Sarah Jane Morris, she's called, a tall woman with red curls, looking at her you can already see that she's going to get very fat and won't give a damn. There is hope, then. If you can sing you can have it all. *Set me free / set me free / set me free* . . . She lets her voice go, until the guy in the room to her left pounds on the wall. Cardboard walls. The outside walls are cardboard too, it's cold in the rooms. Already. It's going to be something this winter. Does that radiator actually work? No idea, she'll find out. Otherwise she'll have to ask the concierge, the big woman who reminds her of Aunt Margarethe. . . . She closes her eyes for a moment. A whole day off. Free all day to do as she pleases. Grandmother Lambert's given her a small vacation bonus, maybe she can buy some clothes. Where do you go to buy something like that in Paris? Definitely not Galeries Lafayette, that's too expensive. . . . Maybe Monoprix, or the French C&A. She could also just take the Metro somewhere, anywhere, she has a *carte orange* now, she can use it to travel the whole month. She was so proud when the Metro clerk slipped the orange card with her passport photo on it into the plastic cover and slid it to her in the tray under the window. It was her ticket for the next month, a magical Metro ticket you didn't throw away but always put back in the cover, just like the other Parisians who did it so casually, card out, into the turnstile, flop and straight back into the folder. . . . She had become a resident. *Set me free / set me free / set me free-hee-hee.* . . . She could also drop in on that guy who gave her his address last week, the musician in the Metro. She'd stood there watching a band for a while, they were really good, and one of them soon spotted her. Eye contact, they clicked. He was good-looking in a musician kind of way, craggy and a bit messy, long hands, a cigarette dangling from the corner of his mouth. They chatted a little. He'd lived in Berlin for a while, his German was cute. He gave her his address and phone number. Can you just drop in on someone here, was she brave enough for that? She could also have another look at the place where they were playing, he said it was their regular spot. The day is gray, but she is free, why not? You hear about the attacks and stuff, but she can't read the papers well enough to keep up with all the things that are happening. Of course, there's always something happening in a city this big, you hear a lot of sirens, but there are people everywhere and she never goes anywhere dangerous. She'll tell her mother that again tonight when she calls her, every Wednesday evening from the phone booth at Porte Maillot, she can afford to use up half a telephone card each time. . . .

⸺

WHEN ELOÏSE COMES OUT it's almost noon. Philippe parked his car in the street at nine and has been watching the front door of his parental home ever since; his neck is stiff and the ache in his left shoulder has returned. He starts when the girl finally appears; evidently she slept in. He waits until she's almost reached the end of the street, then gets out of the car, closing the door with a soft click, and follows her on foot. Denim jacket, denim skirt, a black-and-white bandanna tied around her reddish hair; she'll be easy to keep sight of despite being so short. She looks more grown-up than when she comes to work.

She stops at the boulangerie in Rue Pergolèse. Philippe turns, retraces his steps for a moment, then starts following her again when she walks on to the Metro, taking a bite of a croissant. The woman who works at the bakery, adjusting the window display, recognizes Philippe as he passes and greets him, but he doesn't raise his hand. Eyes on the goal. Eloïse skips down the Metro stairs like the child she still is. This is where Philippe ended his pursuit on previous days, but now, wearing tennis shoes and with a ticket in his hand—prepared this time—he carries on after her. Through the turnstile, and into the train car next to the one she boards. He takes up position near the doors between the cars and watches her through the grimy windows. Thank God, she's sat down with her back to him. Not reading, she stares into space and gets up when Châtelet is approaching.

Oh no, not Châtelet. The maze. Philippe worms his way out through the now packed Metro car just in time to see her take the direction of the connection to Porte d'Orléans. Her bandanna plunges into the flow of heads, the number of people making it both easier and more difficult to follow her. On the escalator she suddenly rises up above the crowd, clearly visible, almost too close. He slows his pace for a moment before stepping onto it as well, then has to hurry again not to lose her at the top. He's thirsty, but doesn't dare to stop for one of the bottles of water the mustachioed Pakistani vendors have stacked in pyramids. Up and down they go, through the network of corridors laid out here according to an incomprehensible pattern, the beating heart of the Parisian Metro system, the place where eight main arteries have been sewn together by a brutal surgeon.

Just past one of the endless travelators, where Philippe is catching his breath while calmly gliding along behind Eloïse, the au pair stops and joins a group of people listening to three musicians. A guitarist, a singer with a double bass, and a saxophonist are capitalizing on the midday crowd, the stream of wallets heading out to or returning from lunch. A corner in the corridor is good for the acoustics, the bass player's voice carries well, and the small amp on a trolley does the rest. Eloïse seems to know the guitarist; he greets her with a smirk on his bony face. She stands next to the small group of tourists, takes the cloth off her head, and shakes out her hair, swaying to the music: Van Morrison, the Beatles, Bob Dylan, a feeble repertoire the trio still manages to instill with a little fire, or at least familiarity; the clink of change falling into their hat sounds regularly. Philippe dawdles, goes back down the corridor— thank God he finds a small store full of knickknacks where he, keeping half an eye on the group a little farther along, is able to take a very long time over the purchase of a plastic robot for Nicolas. By the time the group packs up, it's almost one thirty.

To Philippe's astonishment, Eloïse stays with the group, talking to the guitarist, twisting her thick hair around her fingers. He's never seen her like this before. The boy, actually more a man in his late twenties, touches her. His hand resting on the middle of her back for a moment, on her arm, brushing her cheek with a finger. She submits readily, alternating her weight on her left and right foot in contrapposto, letting her backpack dangle from one hand, laughing with her head back, accepting a cigarette. Philippe sees her smoke for the first time. He's disappointed in her.

The group takes the Metro with Eloïse in tow. They get onto line 4; as a group they're easier to follow and Philippe feels confident enough to board the same car. He no longer wonders what he's doing, he doesn't wonder if they are starting to get worried about his absence from work at faraway Renault.

There is only the here and now.

It is still busy. There is some whispering between the three musicians while Eloïse stares at the black, reflective window; from a distance it looks like they're divvying up the money. Now the bass player stands up. He quickly peels the cover off his instrument, takes up position in front of the doors, and launches into "Under the Boardwalk," to the approval of the tourists in the car, who are in high spirits after a couple of glasses of lunchtime wine. People reach into their pockets for coins. The skinny guitarist takes the porkpie hat off the back of his head and does a round; fortunately Eloïse stays where she is and continues chatting to the saxophonist, as relaxed as if she's catching a train through Southern Germany with her family.

The guitarist is suddenly close by, Philippe has nowhere to go with his back to the wall of the car. The man has a brazen, acne-scarred face, the charm of Mick Jagger. He pokes Philippe in the stomach with his greasy hat. "P'tite pièce pour la musique, m'sieur?" Philippe feels like he's choking, fumbles in his wallet, can't find anything small, then tosses a hundred-franc note on top of the coins. A twisted grin. "M'ci 'sieur." As the guitarist walks back jangling the hat, Philippe sees him quickly slip the note into his back pocket.

ELOÏSE AND THE GUITARIST are now alone, having separated from the other two while changing at Montparnasse-Bienvenüe. Philippe thinks he's lost sight of them for a moment, then spots her hair and his hat just in time as they're getting onto line 13, only to get off again at Gaîté, one stop later. Philippe, not used to taking the Metro and definitely not this far, feels like he's emerged from a stagnant pond once they're outside again. On Avenue du Maine the jackhammers of urban renewal are banging away. He walks behind the couple for a few streets, the man now regularly resting his hand on the back of Eloïse's neck, under her thick hair. He's not wasting any time. In Rue Raymond Losserand, where nineteenth-century tenements of three or four stories alternate with cheap modern buildings, they shoot into a bar with aluminum-framed windows, lotto results stuck to the dirty glass. Philippe doesn't know what to do, but when he sees them sitting at a table with two beers, fries, and a plate of sausages, he knows they'll be a while. The sudden relaxation gives him time to notice his rumbling stomach, parched throat, and the thin steel band being drawn tight around his head. It's three o'clock and no benches in sight. He kills half an hour with a bag of peanuts and a can of Coke from a nearby store, dawdles for a while in front of a copy center and a dry cleaner's, then studies a small bookstore's window display. *Où Va la France?* is the title of a book arranged in a fan shape with multiple copies. The cover shows a well-known news photo of the attack on the Paris-Lyon high-speed train, framed by a torn tricolor. The bookseller has really worked hard on his display, with a wrinkled flag as the background and various front pages of the previous month's attacks draped around it. He must have been planning it for a while, deliberately saving the newspapers to use them as decorations.

When Philippe looks up, Eloïse and the musician are emerging from the bar and he sets off after them, much to the disappointment of the bookseller, who thought he'd spotted a customer.

ELOÏSE IS HAVING DOUBTS. The boy, well, the man, Jean is his name, has invited her in. They're at the door of a building in a narrow street, she doesn't actually have a clue anymore where she is. Near Montparnasse, that brown colossus, yes, she knows that much. She likes him, definitely, but it's going a bit fast. Just then, for a moment, with the others, it felt like she'd found a group of friends for the first time since coming here. Now she's alone with Jean, who jokes around with her, *la petite Allemande*, and keeps touching her. She finds it pleasant but also exciting, it's new, men always call out all kinds of things to her but they never pay her any real attention. They never really talk to her, they never gently rest a hand on her arm, on her back. Would she like to come in for a bit? It's a friend's apartment. He's staying here for a couple of months to play some music in the city for a while. He can play something else for her, if she likes. She has a nice voice, they can jam a little. Her cheeks are warm from the large beer, she's not used to drinking in the middle of the day like this. Jean wraps his guitarist's hand around her soft shoulder once again. You're really pretty, you're so different, that beautiful hair, your skin, you're not miserable the whole time like French girls. You surprised me there in the Metro,

I hadn't expected you. You're a real daredevil, come in, don't worry. We'll just play a bit of music. . . . Eloïse tugs on her denim skirt, picks at her bag, her hair. The guitarist types in a code to open the door and takes her by the hand. She follows him over the threshold.

PHILIPPE WAITS.

He feels like things aren't going according to plan, that something's wrong—but he doesn't know what. She has got away from him, he saw her hesitate before going into the apartment building; should he have prevented it? Should he have come rushing up, like a jealous husband on the lookout? No. Now that he's listening to his fears, they spur him on toward a still unknown destination. All he can do is keep watch. Fortunately, there's a bench some fifty yards farther along on the other side of the street.

He waits. Even if it takes all day and all night, he has to wait until she reemerges. Until the shadow of danger is not only impending but within reach. Until *the moment has come*, whichever moment that might be. He runs his hand over his damp face, which is hot and cold at once, like a dewy field. He could sleep for hours, but he could also stay awake for days on end if that's what it takes.

He waits. He is a guard, a sentinel, an immobile bearskin hat like the ones he once saw at Buckingham Palace, on vacation with his parents. He is a lion on a pillar, a three-headed Cerberus.

WHEN ELOÏSE COMES OUT again more than an hour later, she is alone. Her movements are slow. Philippe jumps up and walks a bit farther down the street to watch her from behind an advertising column.

She stands on the street and looks around. Even from a distance, Philippe can see that her face, so radiant before, is now ashen.

She walks, seemingly disoriented. She sits down on the bench where Philippe was sitting, opens her backpack, and pulls out a hairbrush. With long strokes, she starts brushing her hair. It's like she can barely lift her arms. Then she pulls out the bandanna and wipes her face; she must have been crying. She wipes her eyes again, then ties the cloth around her hair once more and sits there with her face in her hands, her elbows resting on her knees and the black-and-white Converse All Stars on her feet turned toward each other, white toes almost touching.

A hobo walks by with a rattling pushcart, shreds of paper blow out of the open bulk bags quivering inside it. Two women with their hair up pass, folders clasped in front of their chests, the heels of their pumps clicking. A man with a dog, two boys grabbing at each other, thumping each other, laughing. Nobody sees the au pair.

A small red book now emerges from Eloïse's pack; Philippe recognizes the Paris street directory. She leafs through it, even the pages seem heavy. Eloïse looks up, leafs through it some more, studies a page. Then she stands up and starts walking, as if shuffling through loose sand, in the direction of Tour Montparnasse. It has just gone four thirty.

SOMEWHERE DEEP WITHIN PHILIPPE a tension starts growing, something inside him is being cranked tighter and tighter. From the moment he saw her come back out, he has known that he has failed at something. And although he doesn't know what—he suspects it, but doesn't want to admit the words—it mustn't happen again. It should never have happened.

FROM NOW ON HE can't make any more mistakes.

He is now walking a hundred feet behind Eloïse, neither more nor less, as if they're linked by a cord that cuts straight through the crowd. Eloïse rediscovers something of her usual pace, but keeps her head down. Via Avenue du Maine, slaloming around the road menders, she heads for Tour Montparnasse. To Philippe's relief she doesn't go in, but carries on straight ahead, along the crowded Rue du Départ, where they both have to suddenly wade through office workers, backpackers, and people with cheap suitcases; employees from the tower, and tourists, fresh from the station, looking for a cheap hotel in its shadow. They cross the raceway of Boulevard du Montparnasse, his movements seem to echo hers. Eloïse is bumped by a man in a tremendous rush who also sideswipes Philippe; Eloïse stumbles over a hole in the asphalt sidewalk, a moment later Philippe catches his foot in the same hole.

They turn right, onto Rue de Rennes.

ALL KINDS OF THINGS could intervene now. A red light. Someone asking directions. A shop window catching her attention. A minute, half a minute, a few seconds would be enough, marking time for a moment, stopping the film.

But that doesn't happen.

AT FIVE O'CLOCK ELOÏSE crosses the road to the Tati clothing store. *TATI les plus bas prix*. The poor man's Lafayette. Philippe could have known. The sagging fabric, the poor fit, and the bad taste— yes, this is where this girl must go to get herself a new outfit; the salary his mother pays her is bound to be modest. Unsure whether he should go in as well, he finally decides to wait on the other side of the street until she comes back out. He's hot, his temples are throbbing, his feet are burning in the tennis shoes that have never covered this many miles before. Philippe waits.

Five past five, ten past five. The pain in his shoulder is almost unbearable, he is now holding his left arm tight with his right hand.

The shameful image he kept seeing on vacation looms up: him, hugging the girl tight while they roll over the ground together. . . . He shudders: After a gust of warmth, a metallic chill now passes through his body. Thirteen past five. The traffic surges along Rue de Rennes to the rhythm of the traffic lights. It's almost rush hour, soon the long artery from Saint-Germain-des-Prés to Montparnasse will be blocked and it will stay that way until twilight, the red and white lights forming two long strands in the growing dark. Fourteen past five. Philippe feels that his legs want to move but they can't, his feet stuck in a lump of unyielding matter.

Quarter past five.

Eloïse comes out again. In her hand a plastic bag with the familiar pink check and the big blue cowboy letters, TATI, he can read it from across the road. She still looks pale. She walks, no, shuffles past the boxes where the brightly colored sale items are piled high, chaotic after a Wednesday afternoon of being grabbed and judged by countless hands. Then she stops on the sidewalk next to a garbage container, close to the traffic lights and the crosswalk. Her head is hanging. She looks in the bag and pulls out something white, patting her eyes with it. She takes a receipt out of the bag and throws it in the garbage container. It's like she's glued to the spot, what's got into her? Philippe talks to her: "It's green, start walking, go, come on." He feels his back curling, a bow that's being drawn. The pedestrian light changes color again.

Sixteen past five.

Eloïse takes out her red book again, now probably looking for the closest Metro station so she can go home. Philippe hopes so and he doesn't hope so, all the way back again and this whole day has been pointless. That can't be it, it can't be. All this has to be for something.

Seventeen past five.

A woman sees Eloïse looking through her book, a woman with black frizzy hair dressed in a white two-piece. She asks her something, offers to help, points to something on the page, then points in the direction of Montparnasse. Yes, you could catch it there, but you could also keep on walking. Look, she points, Saint-Placide is just up there. . . . Eloïse nods, slowly, she still doesn't seem to be all there. It's turned green again and now it's back to red.

Eighteen past five.

"Eloïse!" Her name escapes him like vomit.

"Eloïse!"

—

SHE LOOKS UP, a flash, a split second of blind incomprehension. Then she recognizes her employer across the road. It's weird, so impossible in this place and time that it simply can't be true. But he refuses to disappear.

What's he doing here? He looks terrible, a face like smeared saliva, wearing a weird jacket, white shoes. Sneakers, in the daytime? Shouldn't he be at work? He's holding his arm as if it's broken and he's screaming something, she thinks he's screaming her name. It is so outside the order of things, it's disturbing. She'd like to walk away, but that would be strange too, walking away from her boss. Everything is so nasty, so strange, she should never have gone inside with that Jean, she's doing her utmost to shut out what just happened—and now this too. She clasps the plastic bag with the new underpants in her hand. She wants this day to stop, she wants this day to never have happened, she wants to go to her room, she wants to go to her mother. She wants to go home.

—

NINETEEN PAST FIVE AND the light is red again but it has to happen now.

Philippe tears his feet free from the viscous mud of the sidewalk and starts to cross Rue de Rennes through the traffic. He runs, stumbles, tries to force his legs to take giant steps, but as if it's a dream, the steps die before they're fully formed. A taxi beeps, a red Dyane brakes, he hops, jumps, and falls across the wide street, just next to the pedestrian crossing, reaches the sidewalk, the wide sidewalk close to where dumbstruck Eloïse is still standing, motionless, her green eyes wide and scared, the plastic bag screwed tight in her hand. Philippe lets go of his left arm, the pain is immense, a roaring in his ears, three more steps and he's reached her. Three steps.

Twenty past five.

He spreads his arms, not Cerberus but an octopus, he spreads his arms and legs, the convulsions of the first months of his life course through his adult body, and he throws himself at Eloïse, who is now screaming. He drags her back ten or fifteen feet with the first impact, stumbling along, then wraps himself around her as he hurls himself farther, they roll another ten feet, no, they hit the ground together, and then there's the bang. The blow.

The thud.

AN ENORMOUS, DEAFENING, BLINDING pressure wave. A massive block of air, hitting them like a truck, hurling them together against the front of the clothing store, entangled with metal boxes and towels and T-shirts and bath mats and socks and covered with a cloudburst of broken glass.

IT'S TRUE WHAT THEY say, the way it's described by passersby, the ones who live to tell the tale. All at once:

you can't see

you can't hear
you can't feel.

⌒

THE ATTACK ON TATI in Rue de Rennes is the deadliest of that month in Paris and of the year 1986: seven fatalities and between fifty-two and fifty-five wounded. The numbers vary. Was the bomb thrown from a passing car? Had it been planted in the garbage container? That too varies. So messy, the whole history is messy and the attacks most of all, because who can keep a clear perspective when faced with a mountain of bricks, glass, twisted metal, plastic, limbs, blood, splintered bones, bags, stray shoes, with more and more cars cramming into the street as if off a production line that hasn't been shut down yet, the ambulances that have to make their way between them, a Korean camera crew that happened to be the first on the scene, police cars stopping crisscross on the street, men with walkie-talkies jumping out of them, men with bulletproof vests, women with their duty weapons drawn; tatters and shreds and splashes and splinters, is it bone, is it food, is that brains, is it paper, fabric, skin, metal, are they teeth? Who can keep a cool head, who is still able to look, note, consider, deduce, record?

This attack involved the same kind of homemade bomb as the previous ones and is claimed by the CSPPA, the Comité de Solidarité avec les Prisonniers Politiques Arabes et du Proche-Orient. A branch of Lebanese Hezbollah demanding the release of three terrorists, along with an end to French support for Iraq in its war with Iran.

There is no link between these concepts and the people on the street, between the goal of the group and the dead and wounded and the dying who are being flown to hospitals by helicopter in a futile attempt to save them. It simply doesn't exist.

Maybe a link will be laid at some stage, a link to the future. Words that stick, words that grow larger. Perpetrators who still have to be born. They constitute an ongoing thread that will be embroidered into the fabric of time, forming a winding pattern through the 1980s, the 1990s, the 2000s, the 2010s—a pattern that can only be perceived in retrospect, stitch by stitch by stitch.

IF ELOÏSE HAD STAYED where she was, next to the garbage container, she would have been fatality number eight and Philippe a living, unscathed witness. Now they sink together into the anonymous morass of the wounded. The group that can count on two, maybe three weeks of attention: But there are already so many this month, this year, these days. Later a few of them will get a name, a face, because they've written a book and appear—leaning on a stick or with thick makeup that can't quite conceal the scars from their burns—on talk shows.

PHILIPPE AND ELOÏSE ARE both unconscious. It will take a few hours to establish their identities and reach their relatives: This is the eighties. A paramedic sitting next to Philippe on the way to Hôpital Sainte-Anne finds a business card in his pocket. Laurence doesn't have the faintest suspicion until the telephone rings; Philippe told her he might be late. Besides some bruising, he has virtually no external injuries but is in a coma because of the cerebral hemorrhage caused by the blow.

Eloïse's mother is waiting that evening for her daughter's weekly telephone call while *Tagesschau* shows the first images of the ambulance-packed, red-and-blue-flashing Rue de Rennes. In the meantime, Eloïse's *carte orange* has been fished up out of the inside pocket of the denim jacket they cut off her in Hôpital Paris Saint-Joseph. She has a fractured skull, a collapsed lung, a crushed left arm, broken ribs, a perforated stomach, a damaged kidney that will be removed that night, a broken hip, and a left knee that has been smashed to jelly. As soon as it is medically responsible, her family has her brought back to Germany. Away from Paris.

THE DOCTORS OPERATE AND the family hopes and prays. Eloïse's mother sits by her daughter's bed in the Universitätsklinikum Tübingen and knits sock after sock after sock. She curses France, curses Paris, curses the day she registered her daughter at the au pair agency. Her despair is unchanneled, it has nowhere to go and rages through her body and her tormented mind.

In Paris, Ghislaine goes to the Notre Dame des Victoires every morning and sinks to her knees before Saint Thérèse to beg for the recovery of her youngest son. Like tens of thousands before her, she promises a plaquette to the Virgin or any saint at all who will listen to her, taking comfort from the off-white marble plates with red inscriptions that cover the church's walls and columns. Their words echo down through the years. *Merci à Marie 1916, Merci Ste Rita, Reconaissance à Jesus et Marie 1948, Merci à St. Antoine 1890, À Dieu et Marie Merci, Remerciement à St. Joseph, Nous avons invoqué Marie / Elle a sauvé notre enfant / Août 1867.* Every day Ghislaine chooses a different one, fixes her eyes on it, and stares hard until tears flow, thinking: A miracle must be possible, people have been invoking miracles here for two hundred years. I have to try too, it's possible, it is possible.

LAURENCE SITS AT PHILIPPE'S bedside, holds his hand now and then, and wonders how well she knows this man. She has so many questions, but it's too soon for that, or perhaps too late. What Philippe was doing there. At that hour. In tennis shoes. Where the au pair came from, without underwear. How it was possible that they were found there welded together, like lovers under the ash of Pompeii.

⌒

PEOPLE NEED MIRACLES. AFTER a few weeks Eloïse opened her eyes and lived on. The au pair agency informed the Lambert family of the girl's tentative improvement. Laurence bought a card with a picture of a flowering mimosa on it, wrote a message wishing her a complete recovery, and lied that Nicolas still sometimes asked after her. Then she closed the dossier "Eloïse" in her mind, which was troubled enough without it.

THAT'S ALL I KNOW about Eloïse. I do know how Philippe emerged from all this, Flo, because three years later, after I had run away from our story, he became my employer.

II

Marie's Story

1989

1

I PUT DOWN MY suitcase and pressed the top button. The reflection in the large pane of glass behind the wrought iron bars made no bones about it: hair hacked off as hurriedly as my jeans—now shorts—scrawny arm protruding from an old C&A T-shirt. Faded sneakers, cheap suitcase, yep, all typical. The plastic Walkman. This was no way to arrive in Paris, I saw that too, but what was the right way? First there was the dirty, tacky train and then the Metro, then the illogical streets with continuous facades like the walls of a maze. This was the right street, it was the right number, and in the glass I could see the ghost ringing the bell. It was August 18, 1989, a date with lots of eights.

THE HEAVY DOOR GAVE way with a metallic click. I lifted my foot over a high doorstep and put it down on the mosaic tiles of the vestibule, green leaves on a white background. The door closed, the street noise disappeared. The next door, glass in oak, didn't have a panel with numbers but it did have a bell, which rang loudly. Everything here was different.

The concierge opened the door. Her blank face appeared first and studied me through the glass. The face was attached to a rectangular body in a smock. She was big, a strapping woman with bottle-blond hair and a mop in one hand. If I'd had any expectations, I would have thought, *so* un-French, but I didn't have any. The floor of the long, dark hall behind her was wet and gleaming. She looked at me, eyes moving up and down over the mess that I was, and said, "Ah, la Hollandaise."

She disappeared into a cubbyhole to the right of a large, leisurely stairwell with an open elevator shaft in the middle, and reappeared with two keys, an envelope, and a note with numbers on it (*"Le code"*). She seemed to say something about a door and a room, "trois A," then showed me the way to the back. Down a narrow hallway and out of the building, across the courtyard, through a yellow door, then seven flights up a narrow, wooden spiral staircase. Up to the eighth floor with the suitcase banging against the steps. A long hall with doors close together on both sides; the key really did fit 3A. Why was I surprised? In the room I opened the small window and collapsed on my back on a lumpy bed, lying there until dusk did what it does all over the world: paint the walls.

IT WAS ALMOST DARK when I came to. I drank disgusting water from the faucet above the small sink and descended the seven floors on the spiral staircase for the first time. In flip-flops now, but still wearing the same clothes, catching a whiff of my travel-worn body on the rising draft. I crossed the shady inner courtyard, then the dark hall, where a light flicked on, pulled my new, heavy front door open, and walked out with the key in my hand. The air was thick. August was the month from hell, the heat off the paving stones clasped my ankles.

Left, right, then suddenly a large thoroughfare. In the distance I saw a tall, brightly lit building, a congress center on a large traffic circle, a neutral tableau that could be found in any city. Porte Maillot. Good enough to start with. I walked toward it and the sidewalk grew wider, the streets got wider too and a little cooler, the evening sky opened up.

I stood at the traffic circle for a while, watching the traffic hurl itself around it with neither discipline nor logic. The roar and stench were everywhere. I could have stood there for hours without anyone paying me the slightest bit of attention. Just standing there, a mooring post in the flood of people, dust, and soot. A little bit of space began to grow—no bigger than a beechnut, but still—in my flat chest and in my throat and in my head. I think it was this: the realization that I didn't know anyone here at all, that nobody saw me and nobody spoke my language. And that, for now, was just what I needed.

I took a right and then another, and felt a tremendous sense of relief at the sight of my own street sign, as if both street and building could have evaporated in my absence. At the late-night store across from the front door, I bought a loaf of bread, a bottle of water with a lump of ice in it, cigarettes, and a bag of dates.

THAT WAS THE FIRST day, at least: That was the day as recorded. I jotted down loose words on a sheet of A4 paper, the next day again, and after that, again. Not thoughts or sentences, just loose words as remnants of the day. I laid the sheets of paper in a plastic box I found at the bottom of the only wardrobe, which smelled of old clothes. Later the box moved with me to all the addresses I would live at. When I recently opened it to tell you this story, Flo, the paper still carried that same smell.

2

I COULDN'T NAME A single street, route, tree, or face from those first few days. The city was flickering hot, I do remember that. I went out, looked for a supermarket, bought a newspaper I couldn't read. I slept. I ate bread and fruit and drank water and wandered aimlessly, increasing my radius. I got used to the palette: bluish gray and off-white, surroundings the color of pebbles, framed by wrought iron curls. At the end of the day, I blew my nose in smooth pieces of pink toilet paper and black gunk came out. I didn't feel any weariness, but slept in my baking attic room as if unconscious. There was no connection between the things I did or saw, except that they were all happening in the period that extended until I started work. When I looked back, I didn't see anything, and definitely not you, Flo, and looking ahead I didn't see anything either. I existed.

I HAD WORKED OUT from the note the concierge had given me that my working life would not be taking place where I lived, and took the Metro to meet the family, who had recently moved southwest of the inner ring. Only the family's grandmother, Ghislaine Lambert, recently widowed, lived in the building where my room was located, in an apartment on the fourth floor. She was the one who paid me, lending, as it were, her maid to her son. This was the first of many surprises, one of numerous details that didn't fit in the twenty-five-word ad that appeared in English in the *Algemeen Dagblad*.

> Paris. Nice working family (2 boys, 6&1 yrs) seeking reliable, quiet au pair girl (Dutch/German, 17–23 yrs) from August 15–July 15. Regular working hours+pay, housing+transport+languagecourse incl.

I kept the ad. It could have been any city, any country, as long as it wasn't the Netherlands. I didn't need any more words.

I CHOSE A METRO exit by random and started walking in the wrong direction. A situation that would occur frequently in the city and invariably made me feel a little queasy, as if I had stepped into a reflection. I turned back and ran to the apartment building, a 1960s block with a parking lot surrounded by rustling poplars. The entrance hall was lined with dark wood, the small elevator had smoked glass mirrors. In the elevator, I repeated the names: Laurence and Philippe Lambert. The children: Nicolas and Louis. Laurence, Philippe, Nicolas, Louis.

On the seventh floor the mother opened the door, Laurence. A small woman with a sharply cut bob, wearing a sleeveless blouse with a large bow. Under it, a pair of shiny briefs. Muscular legs, like a dancer in the days of flappers. She went up onto her toes to greet me with kisses left and right, close to my ears, while holding the hand with her cigarette stretched away from me. "*I ham so glad you are 'ere*," she said, and immediately launched into a tour of the apartment.

I had never seen a home so small before. Immediately in front of the door, one step across the tiny entrance hall: the kitchen, stacks of appliances taking up all available space. To the right, two steps along the hall, a very small room on the left with two children's beds pushed together. One step farther: the master bedroom, filled entirely with a double bed. On it lay the father, a pale man with a lock of hair across his forehead. He raised a hand without looking at me.

Turn right: bathroom. Right again: the toilet. This was hung from ceiling to floor with dark rose wallpaper and it was the only room with a door. The other doors had undoubtedly been removed to save space. The living room, left of the front door, was filled with a sofa that was draped with a sheet of floral material, a tanker-like sideboard with a cut-glass mirror, and a round oak table. No bookcase—I remember how much that surprised me. Nowhere in the whole apartment could you take more than seven uninterrupted steps.

Ten minutes after the mother opened the door, she had completed her tour, told me what they were having for dinner and how the microwave worked, demonstrated the tricky faucet in the bathroom, shown me where to find diapers and pajamas, and pulled on a tube skirt and light yellow pumps while continually walking to and fro, talking in French and repeating it all in something that resembled English. In the living room she bent down quickly and gracefully to kiss the two children I only now noticed. Then she left with the father, who still hadn't said a word to me. A good-looking couple. Even that very first time, I had been astonished by their ability to depart from this rabbit hole impeccably dressed, trailing their smoke and perfume behind for me, Cinderella.

The oldest boy was sitting under the table acting out a pileup with his toy cars. The youngest one was crying loudly in a playpen that was jammed between the table and the wall. They both had round, brown, frightened eyes. I felt clumsy and sweaty and had forgotten their names. Nothing I had ever learned was of any use to me in this moment.

THEY SURVIVED. Nicolas and Louis. They even ate something (canned green beans and steak I ruined on the hot plate), and the little one calmed down at some stage of the evening. He had soft chestnut hair and was only just walking. Once the two of them had settled in bed—like me, in a state of shock—and fallen asleep, I took a bath. For the first time in a week I was able to completely wash myself in a bath, albeit one that was scarcely bigger than a mortar tub. After cautiously lowering myself into the water, I had to cry for a moment. Because of everything, Flo.

THE FATHER INSISTED ON giving me a ride home. He'd been drinking but the last Metro had already left. Silently, with his foot flat to the floor of his Renault, he tore through tunnels and along the ring road. While the lights flashed by—you know how that yellow light fans out in a windshield at night—I realized it was the first time I was driving through this new city, an old city that was now my new city. For the first time, the first time, the first time.

When the father, Philippe, dropped me off in front of the building he'd grown up in, he spoke to me directly for the first time, in perfect English. *"You are not as young as the other girls."*

3

THE LANGUAGE, HOW DID it go with the language at the start? Ads, billboards, stray business cards, labels, street signs, instructions— as many letters as bricks, as many words as people, and they all demanded to be read, deciphered, understood, obeyed.

For the time being, I guessed. I guessed that they wanted me to open an account at Paribas, take a course, get ready for "the *rentrée*." Not sit on the lawn, buy lingerie for the fall even though it was still eighty-five degrees, get myself a monthly ticket. Medium Soufiane offered her services for all problems. I spelled out the words, turning them over and over in my mouth, speculating.

The spoken language was a different matter. That was a wall. Conversations around me were made up not of words but of sounds smeared together. Vowels, consonants, syllables—an enthusiastic bricklayer had made it his masterpiece. Where was the door? How could I get past it? I might just as well have been deaf, or a dog. No, a dog would have understood more. Sometimes the father, Philippe, would invite me to watch *Questions pour un Champion* with him, "good for your French." He'd have just got home, changed from one ironed shirt into another ironed shirt (I knew that, I had to iron them), and was slumped on the crumpled *grand foulard*, the cloth over the sofa, joining in with the quiz.

The host was called Julien Lepers, a thickly made up man who spoke like a machine gun. If I tried hard, I could get the contestants' names and the town they came from. Daniëlle from Jura. Brigitte from Dijon. Jean-Luc from La Rochelle. Was the father being sadistic or just exercising a perverse sense of humor with the quizzical looks he gave me before answering the questions himself? I still had to get to know him; it would take a while.

I PRACTICED. FOR INSTANCE, the "*bonjour*" you were expected to blurt out on entering each and every store. *Bonjour. Bonjour.* Bon*jour* (high-low). *Bon*jour? (low-high). *Bonsh.* The "*BONN-SHEWER*" American tourists blared at the Metro ticket office with enviable aplomb.

Now and then I would pry a brick out of the wall. A *carnet*: a booklet of ten Metro tickets. A *glace* was an ice cream but also a mirror. *Une pression*: a beer. *Chez vous*: your place. I knew the days, I could give my name, I could count, I could call the two boys over to me. I had to dredge the words up from my high school days, a time that felt light-years away. Somebody else's past.

I GOT USED TO the view from my room, a narrow rectangle framed by the small bay window, a tiny part of the sea of grayish-blue zinc roofs. The flock of pigeons circling over those roofs was the first cliché I embraced. The Palais des Congrès was my beacon in the distance. In the evening light flowed up and down the congress center in a show that ended at exactly ten o'clock, suddenly and sometimes in mid-sequence, as if somebody inside had pulled the plug.

My street was quiet but never silent. I could always hear someone walking, the click of heels, the hoses of the street cleaners in the morning. Sometimes I heard people talking on the sidewalk. The acoustics of the narrow street sucked the sound up and deposited it gently on my windowsill and I liked that, it took the edge off the loneliness.

I leaned out of the window and smoked cigarettes, red Gauloises from the swindler across the road. I didn't smoke for the taste, but because it felt like a decision that had nothing to do with anybody else. Including you, Flo. I smoked, looked out over the blue roofs— *bonjour, bon*jour? bon*jour!*—and dropped the butt in the gutter.

4

WHY DID PEOPLE DO this, entrust their children to a complete stranger and a terrified one at that? They were mad. But I was here now and I couldn't pass the task on to anyone else.

To reach the playground, you had to cross a large road. A droning gully with enormous behemoths steamrolling through it. I let the first couple of green lights come and go. A lady looked back at us. I couldn't stay there forever. I squeezed the oldest boy's hand so hard he started yelling *aïe, aïe, aïe* (even pain sounded different here). With the other hand I pushed the swerving stroller, in which the youngest was trying to wriggle out of the straps. They were both screeching. We made it to the opposite sidewalk, and when we got to the gate of the playground I realized I was still holding Nicolas in a viselike grip. I relaxed my hand and he shot off.

I had wanted to tell him that the sky would have come crashing down if I'd let go sooner, that the world was full of blind, wheeled constructions that weighed tons. That we might not know each other yet and might not even like each other, I felt that too, but that I couldn't just let him step out in front of a bus. My meager vocabulary didn't stretch to a single one of those phrases and he wouldn't have forgiven me anyway.

A little later I was sitting with the youngest on my lap while the oldest threw sand at another child, but nobody was crying.

Louis turned toward me and gazed at me for a long time with a highly serious expression, suddenly looking very old. Then he laughed, he crowed and reached for my face with his crumb-covered hands and pinched my cheek with peculiar strength. I had achieved something.

THE ROUTINE WAS SIMPLE enough. My workdays started at quarter past twelve, fifteen minutes before Laurence left for work. After entering the apartment I ensconced myself in the kitchen to make sure she had all the available room at her disposal. She walked from the bedroom to the living room, in and out of the bathroom ten times, already in her red Air France uniform.

Her life was so full, her apartment so small, and her husband . . . His role was unclear to me. It was, in any case, insignificant. I pressed myself against the miniature countertop, where the ravages of the morning were waiting for my attention.

Laurence kept flashing by the doorless doorway, smoking and jangling her keys, chattering away without looking at me—talking to me, talking in general, or talking to her sister through a large portable receiver she held wedged between her head and shoulder. I didn't know if I was expected to listen; my tasks were already listed on the note stuck to the fridge door with a magnet and probably written for a previous au pair.

> 1. Tidy 2. Iron 3. Walk Louis + 4. Shopping (see list) + extra
> ironing 5. Nap Louis + afternoon tea 6. 4:30 pm end of
> school day Nicolas 7. Outdoors 8. Cook 9. Tidy. 10. Kids in
> bath.

Afternoon tea, as she demonstrated, was a half baguette with three pieces of chocolate in it. Sometimes she put a note on the table with additional tasks: *Pick up cigarettes (Dunhill extra long). Clean fridge. Go to dry cleaner's. Clean Nicolas's schoolbag.* The last one meant scraping out the tacky candy she threw into it every morning, which he never ate.

NONE OF THIS IS particularly special and yet every detail stuck. I want you to understand, Flo, that I was a cleared table, a wiped blackboard, a section of street where the now departed workers had dug up all the cobblestones to replace the pipes. Not new, not really clean—empty. New impressions were all equally important or unimportant. There was nothing to compare it to, so everything just settled on that empty table, that empty blackboard, that empty stretch of sand. Slowly, slowly a new layer would form on which I might be able to build something, a layer in which contrasts could become apparent. It was still too early for that. I want you to realize that, Flo. To see it before you.

YOU'D HAD SOMETHING ELSE for me in mind. Around this time, when I was cleaning the fridge for people I didn't know, I should have been doing an internship with the photographer who was known for tearing shreds off all his assistants. That counted, the way you described it, as a recommendation. I would learn so much. I would spend days on end printing and lugging lights around and rolling out screens and making calls and getting to know all the sides of our profession the curriculum didn't have room for or ignored because they were too prosaic, although they were the reality. "It will be tough, but believe me, M., it's what you need. You'll meet people who will think of you in the future," that's how you put it. I'd go to openings, drink wine, and meet curators and collectors, maybe have sex with them, you added casually. All those things were going to happen. I'd experience a lot, and that, "for better or worse," was always good.

HARDLY ANY TIME HAD passed since then, but walking from the family's crowded little apartment to the Metro at seven thirty, tired as a mule, on my way to my poky room on the eighth floor, I never gave a second thought to what should have been.

I was here now, this was what I was, and I could only be glad I'd got through another day with these borrowed children in one piece. I had protected them from burns, disease, accidents, starvation, kidnapping, tornadoes, and, my greatest fear, inexplicable disappearance.

5

THE HEAT WAS INESCAPABLE. The streets, buildings, parks, even underground, everything was broiling. At night I dreamed I was sleeping on a griddle. I lived off bottles of water and packs of Super Ed orange juice that I put in the family's fridge and wrapped in newspaper to take home, where they were already lukewarm by the time I had climbed the seven floors. The bareness of the room was an advantage—fewer surfaces to brush against. There was a bed, a small table, a chair. There was a narrow wardrobe with old papers and books stacked on top of it, a dusty pile I didn't touch. Floorboards. A sink with a cabinet above it, a small oval mirror next to it big enough for a face, not a body. On the wallpaper next to that mirror, the previous au pairs had written their names in round, girlish handwriting.

Karin 1983

Natalie 1984

Chantal 1985

Eloïse 1986

Veroniek 1986 (the second that year, something I didn't notice at first)

Astrid 1987

Beate 1988

I added my name: *Marie 1989.*

Finding your feet somewhere is largely a question of copying. At the Lamberts' I used the French press the way I had seen Laurence use it and then, like her, poured the coffee into a bowl and added two sugar cubes. I walked along the street with a loaf of bread wrapped in paper. I spread jam on the bread with a spoon. I wrote on graph paper because they were the only notebooks I could find. I bought a paperback to hold in front of me on the Metro, even though I couldn't read it yet.

The first few weeks I still had the mornings off. At that time of day my street was a cool canyon where the sun only touched the top floors. I took the Metro to Gare du Nord, where I strolled past the sidewalk cafés in the area around the station, looked in through the enormous windows of the bars and restaurants and around me on the street, and tried to distinguish the Parisians from the city's visitors. How could you recognize the locals? How did they sit at tables, how did they hold their cups, what kind of gestures did they make while talking? The French had remarkably little with them and rarely stuffed it into a bag. Men paid with change from their pants pocket. After standing up, women grabbed a stack of paper or books off the tiny table and held it pressed against their chest while walking away on flat shoes, with perfectly straight backs.

Residents hurried without hurrying. They walked fast without running, race-walking along the bitumen-patched sidewalks as if speeding through the smooth corridors of a hospital. Going down the stairs into the Metro, they hardly seemed to touch the steps. Only visitors and tramps and old ladies, who combed their dyed hair up like black cobwebs, maintained a different pace. Visitors installed themselves at the little tables and took a long time over large soup bowls of white coffee. Residents drank their small coffee or morning beer in five minutes at most, standing at the bar. They ate a boiled egg and dropped the shell on the floor, next to the ash from their cigarettes.

I stood on the sidewalk of the short Boulevard de Denain, looking straight at the station, and muttered the names of the cities on its dirty facade. Northern cities you could reach from this station, chiseled into the stone: *Francfort, Amsterdam, Varsovie, Bruxelles.* And, east and west of Paris (in the center, of course): *Londres, Vienne, Berlin, Cologne.* In the seething mass nobody heard my mumbling.

I could have walked straight into the station, past the gray layer of tramps caked around the entrances, and joined one of the long lines at the counters to buy a ticket back to the Netherlands. *Not* doing that was a small victory, which not a single passerby, or even pigeon, noticed.

6

I TRIED NOT TO think about what had gone before, ignoring why I had ended up here. But sometimes a memory suddenly popped up, Flo, and refused to be pushed aside, pressing like a racehorse at a starting gate. Then I'd sit down at the wobbly little table in my room, lay out a 1978 *Paris Match* I'd found in the wardrobe as backing (*"Sophia Loren plus belle que jamais"*), grab a notebook I'd bought here, and start to write.

THE FIRST THING I wrote was this. I called the city we lived in D.:

October, 1987. On Thursday we always have a long practical in the darkroom, it never finishes on time. We come out with our heads floating from the fixer fumes. Then, after a brief detour to the cafeteria, head straight for the bar. I'm nineteen, away from home for six months now, saved by an attentive teacher who said, "Wouldn't something creative be more up your street?" My fellow students have been plucked from other suburbs and housing developments and are glad to finally live somewhere that resembles a city. A few come from larger cities and act like they've ended up in a village. All of us cling to new habits. Thursday, beer day.

It's already getting dark and it's raining. We ride our bikes through the deserted center of D. without lights. I come in through the door, wet

to the skin, and see a tall woman sitting at the bar. A woman with a
pinched nose and eyes that are only half open in a face of pale, smooth
clay. Turned toward me, there's a listless expectation in the way she's
sitting there, as if a show is about to start. She looks me over from head
to toe and says, "Look, a cute little drowned rat."
 That's Flo and she's talking about me. I notice a change in my
group. A ripple, sudden restlessness. The Photography and Film
second-years apparently know this woman; she teaches "narrative
technique," a subject that seems unattainably distant and fascinating.
Somebody mumbles in my ear, "She's really good. But be careful." I
only see her striking, slightly mocking, but also interested face.
Attention, noticeable as a heat lamp. She knows she has that effect, I'm
sure of it. I'm feeling it for the first time. It's like an electric radiator in a
bathroom, you pull the string and the warmth develops like a tangible
presence in the room, descending on your bare shoulders like a sense of
well-being. The woman takes her long cashmere scarf, holds it out with
her telescopic arm, and says, "Dry yourself off. I'll order a beer for
you."
 I don't know what's hit me.

Then I closed the notebook again for a while.

IT WAS ONLY MUCH later, Flo, that I realized I simply met require-
ments. While I thought I was special, singled out, it turned out I
was just sufficient. I was *perfectly normal.* I wasn't overly large, I came
from a hastily erected reconstruction neighborhood. I hadn't had a
distinctly unhappy or happy childhood, I wasn't spoiled but hadn't
grown up poor either. I had a certain degree of talent but no uncontrollable excess, and above all, I had lived until then in the shadows.
You read off the facts as if I'd come with an information leaflet.
 That insight is no use to me now. No matter what I do and how
often I think about it, trying to divert the course of events—I will

still walk into the Duke with dripping hair and a wet jacket, and once again you won't need to turn your clay face toward me because you've been sitting there the whole time waiting for me to stroll into your field of vision. I can't change this scene. The sparrow flew down to the grain and walked under the net.

But I'm getting ahead of myself.

7

PARIS WAS ALL SWINGING doors, like the ones in restaurants in silent movies. Between the front and back, there was almost nothing. Stage and wings, aboveground and underground, present and past—I was continually stepping from one side to the other. It wasn't even stepping, I fell through.

Take living within walking distance of the Arc de Triomphe. In my attic there were twelve servants' rooms—two for each floor—at least that many inhabitants, and one toilet with a cracked bowl that nobody kept clean between us. Across from me, three men from, presumably, India, lived in a room as small as mine. I sometimes bumped into one in the hall, small and slight, giving off a sharp odor of sweat-soaked polyester. One door farther along was a skittish old man whose smoker's cough ripped through the hall in the morning. To my right there was an English couple who argued in the daytime, worked at night, and came home around five in the morning, when they sometimes made love with a mechanical thudding against the wall. I hadn't yet met the others, but our position was clear and it was the same for all of us. We paid, with money or work, too much for small rooms that were too hot in summer and, as I already knew, would soon be too cold in winter. But we weren't locked in. I only had to go down the stairs, across the courtyard, out of the building, right-left-right, and then it was a slightly uphill walk on Avenue de la Grande Armée to the triumphal arch, like Napoleon returning from Austerlitz. A half mile of grandeur, the sound of trumpets, victory. Whatever else, the setting was the same for everyone.

HARD TRANSITIONS, EVERYWHERE. THE father asked me to bring something—a book, nothing special—from his parental home. I was given a key; his mother was away all week and it apparently couldn't wait. The key admitted me to the rear entrance of the fourth-floor apartment, which came out on my spiral staircase. This, then, was the route that, a few lives back, the servant from my room used early in the morning and late at night. I walked down the smooth, worn steps, the key fitted, the code for the alarm was correct, and—I passed through another swinging door.

On the other side it was quiet and shadowy; my footsteps disappeared in thick carpet and the rooms smelled of dusty luxury. The ones left and right of the hall were all open, like in a museum. Wainscoting. Velvet drapes. Chairs and sofas with Gobelin upholstery and thin, crooked legs. Vases that came up to your hips. Cabinets and side tables everywhere.

Hanging in the central hall were four large oil paintings of the Lambert family. Father, mother, three boys, and a girl, all of them good-looking in a casual, privileged way. There, captured in oils, the much younger face of Philippe, in this constellation nothing so much as the youngest son.

In the cramped apartment beyond the ring he seemed like a minor character in the wrong play, invariably awkward when he returned from work before I'd finished cleaning and always doing his best to maintain his distance. Here he was the baby of the family, the favorite son leaning on his mother's knee. Further along, the golden boy of the lyceum. Nowhere in the portraits could I see the large scar that wound from his cheek to his temple and into his hair. That was the advantage of a painting, you could just leave it out. Or maybe he didn't have it yet.

Gleaming around their faces was wood carving with golden curls; in fact, the whole house was hung with gold-painted frames. On the panels of the doors, around the windows, around the bathroom, the kitchen, the dining room, the living room, on the ceilings: a framed life.

I THOUGHT ABOUT THE setting of my own childhood. A 1960s public housing development, low ceilings, single-glazed windows, shared bedroom with wood-chip wallpaper, generic brand jelly, and an oppressive feeling at the end of the month. You know that, Flo. I told you where I come from. Nothing had prepared me for an apartment like this, not even the films you made us watch. Films that were often set in places like this. Where Catherine Deneuve could appear at any moment with a glass in her hand, with her golden blond hair and her large eyelids, slotting into her environment like a piece of a jigsaw puzzle.

You told us that those films were the reality, as Jean-Luc Godard had explained: "Film is truth twenty-four times a second, and every cut is a lie." We believed that, I believed it, I might not have fully understood it, but I still suspected a profound truth within it.

But this was different. This looked like a set in every way, but it was still more real than any film I had ever seen. I ran my hand along the wall as I walked, the ribbing of the relief wallpaper passing under my fingertips. I had taken off my shoes to feel the carpet between my toes.

I found the book easily: in the library, in alphabetical order. I sat down in the leather armchair, then in the other one, then on the sofa as well. I could have left again immediately, I should have left again immediately, but the temptation was too great. While the sofa creaked softly, I thought about Philippe, the father, who had grown up here. Who had been a toddler, a little boy, a teenager. A spoiled adolescent in the heart of the metropolis. With luxurious parties, wine from the cellar, vacations at Cap d'Antibes (I'd heard them talk about their summers). And now he'd been transplanted into a poky little shoebox—with a nanny, but still.

When I gave him the book the next day, he laid it aside without a glance and suddenly I realized what the intention had been: for me to see the apartment. So that his borrowed help knew where he came from.

8

LESSONS STARTED IN SEPTEMBER.

The classroom was in the 5th arrondissement, in a street near the Sorbonne, which sounded impressive but wasn't. It was on the fifth floor of a gray building that could have served any purpose. We gathered in a room like millions of others all over the world and the teacher was the kind of teacher you could have encountered in any of those rooms: Monsieur Dufour. Michel. A brown-haired thirty-something wearing a gray shirt, rimless glasses, not much of a chin.

From the first second, he put his tan lace-up flat to the floor and we tore through the curriculum. Michel Dufour steered the class like a race car driver, never looking around to see if we were feeling nauseous or if someone had failed to take the corner. I sat on the edge of my seat and wrote. I don't know if he was a good teacher, I didn't have time to think about it. The use of the *futur du passé* took up all available brain capacity.

We were five Germans, two Danes, two Swedes, a Spaniard, an Austrian, and me. I was somewhere in the middle, not as young as the DanishGermanSwedes, not as mature as the other two. Spanish Clara was impressive. The camera would have loved the way her profile caught the light, and you would have seen that immediately, Flo. What she was doing in this language class was a mystery to me. Her accent was an intricate, decorative trellis compared to the plow the Germans deployed and the whispered basso continuo of the Danes, who I'd seen knitting in the Metro on the way to class.

Our lack of mastery of the language was the great equalizer. For the teacher, we were all interchangeable; he called on us to speak without looking at us and in alphabetical order. He didn't even notice sculpted Clara, not worth it, in four months there would be new Dutch, Danish, German, and Spanish students, as sure as there were seasons.

On Wednesdays our class moved to a location on Boulevard Saint-Michel above a branch of Caisse d'Épargne. There we were taught phonetics by a gnomelike woman called Josette Deschamps. At the start of the first lesson she looked at us with her small turnip face, then turned to the blackboard, took a piece of chalk, and drew three horizontal stripes.

"This," she said while spinning around to stare at a spot somewhere over our heads, "is the average pitch development through a sentence in your northern languages." She wiped away the end of the lowest stripe and made it curve down instead. "German does have a downward intonation at the end of many sentences, but in general one can safely say that your languages are flat."

Three flat stripes, that was us. I saw Clara raise her hand and then lower it again; her not belonging here wasn't going to distract the teacher. She erased the three stripes and now drew a line like a row of alpine peaks. "This, ladies and gentleman, is how I am going to teach you to speak. French puts demands on your entire range. You don't use it as yet, but you'll learn soon enough."

These hours were the best. I loved the fanaticism of these teachers, their dedication to the language and their contempt for those who didn't share it. Who we were was irrelevant. It didn't matter what we'd been through or what we aspired to. There was no classroom democracy, they weren't interested in us at all, they didn't even pretend to be. The only thing that mattered was our capacity to absorb knowledge. During these mornings we consisted of language and nothing else.

9

MY WEEKS GREW FULLER. I left early for my classes, then went on to the family's apartment, braving the Metro and sometimes a bus. I climbed the stairs and in the evenings I studied or wrote. Or gazed out my window. I was an ant that had discovered a trail of sugar and now followed that route every day with unfailing discipline. You could also call it stupidity, or timidity. This city was full of ants, on every top floor, in every basement, entire satellite towns full of them, places I might visit later. And we all had our tasks, I told myself, we kept the wheels turning. The contrast with the life I had left behind couldn't be greater. In exchange, I had been given a sense of purpose.

If I didn't appear at work, the mother couldn't go to the airport; her plane would be delayed while they arranged a new crew member; a businessman would arrive too late in Hamburg, missing the meeting; the deal wouldn't go through and as-yet-unknown people would miss out on as-yet-nonexistent jobs.

That's what I told myself when I arrived at the family's far-too-cramped apartment, where the workday always began after Laurence's departure with picking up clothes and toys and papers and stray hairbrushes and keys and dirty cups, plates, and saucers. Clearing the pathways, as constrained as they were.

You once showed me the scene in *Una Giornata Particolare*, just after the opening when Sophia Loren wakes everyone and gives them their ironed clothes and coffee. After her husband and children have left for the fascist parade she walks, no, she *strolls* around the apartment. With the lack of sleep showing in her slow movements, she erases the traces of night and morning, pours the remnants of cold coffee into a single cup, and drinks it when she can finally sit down. Have I remembered it correctly? You pulled the video out of your endless *vidéothèque*, put it on, pointed out the brilliance of her gestures, which suggested years of routine—what an actress. Holding that thought while doing my work made it seem not only less futile, it also gave it a kind of beauty.

ONE OF THE PREVIOUS au pairs, Eloïse, had left some clothes behind, Laurence said. Was this any use to me? It was a shapeless thing made of light blue jersey and hung loosely on me, but with a belt it wasn't too bad. It was the first article of clothing that hadn't come with me from the Netherlands, and that felt good, even for an overgrown T-shirt. I put it on, washed it every three days, and hung it on a string in front of the window to dry. You would have rejected it, Flo, but I was discovering the advantages of limited choice. I went out in it one morning and felt that the summer was over its peak. The paving stones were giving off a different smell. There wasn't the same energy in the air. I walked down the street, turned right, turned left, asked for a loaf of bread and paid without thinking, then walked back. For the first time, even after taking the stairs, I wasn't drenched afterward. I only needed to run a washcloth over my neck and I was OK again. The prospect of cool weather and shorter days made the heat less hot.

I PREPARED MY QUESTION in advance, pressed back against the kitchen sink, took a deep breath, and addressed the mother by name. That startled her; I'd never done it before. Abruptly, as if she'd bumped into something, Laurence came to a halt, framed by the doorway. She stared at me from under her dark brown bangs. "Quoi?"

Could they get me a gas burner for in my room? Or a hot plate? She took me in, maybe for the first time consciously. "Pour quoi faire?" To do what? *"You eat 'ere, you drink 'ere . . ."*

To make coffee and tea. To cook on the weekend. "Pour faire la cuisine"—that was the phrase I had prepared.

"Faire la cuisine." She repeated it, chewing over the concept. It seemed that somewhere outside her daily capsule I continued to exist, or attempted to, at least, an attempt she didn't need to engage with, but that now included concrete terms like "making coffee and tea," "weekend," and "cooking." Under that blue shirt my back was getting damp. In the children's bedroom Louis started crying, waking too early from his nap.

"For cooking. Well. Maybe. I will see."

Three days later the concierge handed me a bag containing a dented kettle and two old individual hot plates, one of which turned out to work.

MAYBE THIS IS WHAT you and the other professors and instructors actually meant. We had to be stripped back, you said. Demolished and rebuilt. We had to shuck off the trappings of family, convention, tradition, and customs. We had to become nothing, bare soil, a field that's been weeded and turned. We had to become ourselves, because we weren't yet. We had to unlearn before we could learn, fall silent so we could listen, torment ourselves to console others— we had to do so much. We were being given the opportunity, we had to seize it with both hands.

Everyone used different words but meant the same. And nobody packaged it as beautifully as you, Flo.

You told me, not long after dredging me up, how you had been hiking in the forests of northwestern Spain when an enormous thunderstorm broke. The lightning struck a tree near you. "The leaves all disappeared, the crowns of all the trees, everything around it, it all turned black," you said, "except for the skeleton of the tree that had been hit. I still see that skeleton lighting up, with all of its branches, to the very end of the very last twig. I saw the essence of things there, Marie. That is what I'm looking for, what everyone should be looking for." You were drinking a glass of good red wine. You were a connoisseur of that too and always held the glass by the bottom of the stem. The liquid, ruby colored, swirled around.

I'd never been to northwest Spain. The tree no longer being alive after the lightning strike was something that didn't occur to me.

10

I TRIED TO READ the headlines at the newspaper stand. Something was happening in the world and I had no access to it. It had started in Hungary; a much-reproduced photo showed people flooding through an opening in the barbed wire to cross the border in "*Hongrie*." They were wearing shorts and summer frocks and had nothing with them except their children. The newsdealer chased me off. The mother had no time to talk to me and the speaking tempo on the radio was too fast. Now that I'd been there a month, the father hardly seemed to notice me. He brushed off the question I asked in English: The news didn't interest him and wasn't there always something going on with those communists; should he get excited about that? But when he came home at six he turned the small TV in the living room up to maximum volume before going to lie down in the bedroom to listen to it. Surrounded by the racket of the blaring television, I tidied the room with Louis on one arm while a German minister appeared on a balcony, I think it was the embassy in Prague. He was talking about "*Ausreise*" and "*ab heute*," leaving the country from today. . . . The rest was drowned out by cheers. (Of course I looked this video up again later, in a life with internet. It was just as I'd remembered it.)

I didn't understand any more than the snippets I caught and the great, intangible excitement they conveyed. Until you've mastered a language, events on the world stage take place behind frosted glass.

IN THE EVENING I drilled myself in grammar and vocab and practiced my pronunciation. Our phonetics teacher had launched an assault on the plosive *p* and the wet *f.*

"Your northern languages," she said during a lesson (when she started like that, shame descended over the class, except on the Spaniard), "are too damp and windy." *Beaucoup de vent et d'humidité.* She pulled a candle out of a drawer in her desk, put it on the table, and lit it. "I'm giving you a list of words and a practice sentence. You have to be able to say these words as close as possible to the flame without burning your lips and without"—voice going up, register D—"blowing out the candle." She demonstrated, "Le poivre fait fièvre à la pauvre pieuvre." The flame stood upright like a needle.

The pepper makes the poor octopus feverish. I practiced in my room, without a candle, to the rhythm of the lambada, which someone in one of the rooms down the hall and around the corner kept playing over and over again. I could even hear them rewinding the cassette after it finished. For the first time in months I was overcome by a terrible longing for another body. To lean against. To dance with, mouth to the other's ear, shouting in the crowd, smelling of beer and smoke and fresh sweat.

It was a shock. I ran my hands over my body, which I'd forgotten. I had to relearn that a body could serve for more than just work and being seen. Also that it was more than just words.

THE GIRLS WHO HAD worked for the family before me, had they had bodies? Of course, why not? But try as I might, I couldn't imagine them as living people and the family were no help, they never said anything about the previous au pairs. The oldest boy could probably scarcely remember them, the youngest even less (Nicolas and Louis, I had to start using their names more often, make them more real). Laurence and Philippe knew no past, only haste, and talked to me in instructions and handover information as they'd probably been doing for years. Still, other young women had put their children to bed, entertained them, stroked their silky hair, borne Nicolas's kicking, and also raged at them in their own, foreign language when nobody else could hear. And afterward they were replaced and forgotten, just as I would be replaced and forgotten.

One of them had left something behind, a beer coaster under the table leg—a home improvement. I tried to picture her doing it, imagining somebody else being at home here, pinning photos and maps on the wall, pulling a beer coaster she's brought home from a bar out of her bag and bending to stop the table from wobbling. But all I saw was my own form, seen from outside and above, and even that image soon eluded me.

11

I HAD TO GO to a wedding with them. The mother sent me to a hairdresser for the occasion. Since the dress and the hot plates, she seemed a little more aware of me—a little. She had taken a day off to prepare and I turned out to be one of the things that needed preparing. She had already asked me what I was going to wear, and when I couldn't answer her, she had come up with something for me, undoubtedly her sister's, who was also the bride, and who she was helping through the buildup to the event. A collarless, tapered dress with padded shoulders, pale green with a faint rose pattern. It was hard to imagine anything further removed from what an up-and-coming photographer might wear (you bought me a leather jacket, Flo, I threw it away), but yeah—who knew that here? They could make whatever they liked of me.

Now Laurence was squinting at me from under the bangs she got trimmed every second week. My hair hung down around my neck in long wisps. "Short. Short would suit you," she said. "Good bone structure. *T'en voudrais, des cheveux courts?*" The question as to whether I would like short hair—or was it an order?—confused me for a moment. You thought I should let my hair grow, Flo, and I did. When it was over, I grabbed the kitchen shears. Now I had to have an opinion about it. "Yes, I think so," I said. It turned out she had already made an appointment for me with her own hairdresser, I could go that afternoon. The money was in an envelope.

"Court," I said after sitting in the salon chair, and I raised my hands to my head. And that was what I got. Twenty minutes later, the hairdresser (slim, angular, not very talkative) said, "Voilà, Jean Seberg." I remembered Jean Seberg from your lectures; the heroine of *À Bout de Souffle*, she was found dead in the back seat of her own car. A detail like that is easier to remember than someone's achievements. In the end, that was what the film star became, her hairdo and her tragic death.

Even after paying 120 francs, the exact amount in the envelope, and walking the short distance back to work, I still found it hard to resist raising my hands to cradle my head, it felt so clean and new and delicate. At the apartment, Louis started to laugh and wanted to touch it.

On the Metro on my way back to my room, an elderly lady sitting across from me turned out to be able to see me through her bedewed cataracts after all. "A beautiful cut," she said. "Vos yeux sortent comme des bijoux." Your eyes stand out like jewels.

At a complete loss, I got off at the first stop to wait for the next train.

ON THE DAY OF the wedding I was shuffled between locations. Unwanted at the ceremony, I had to report at the city hall exit afterward. After being crammed into a car and driven to a restaurant in Parc de Saint-Cloud with the youngest on my lap, I was given a place at the lunch table for the children. Seven combed and bashful cousins, plucked out of a Petit Bateau catalog, plus the two who were suddenly very much mine. I had to stay sober, but I had to raise my glass for the toasts too.

The bride—a more robust, pregnant version of Laurence—couldn't stop crying and her brand-new husband looked pale. But he kept touching her, a hand on her neck, her lower back, her forearm. They looked sweet and promising and all at once I realized that I never saw Philippe and Laurence do anything like that at all.

They looked good together but never touched. Even in their tiny apartment, they managed to maneuver around each other like repelling magnetic poles. When he gave her a light, maybe then. They were two solitary, functioning units that happened to have reproduced. Perhaps it was because of Philippe, who stayed on the sidelines even here. It was like the others were avoiding him. In this constellation, mainly his wife's family, his isolation stood out even more: It wasn't just that people were treating him as if he was suffering from an infectious disease, he acted like it too. He stood in a corner, drank hastily, and when someone did speak to him he laughed too loudly, too abruptly, and took a step back. In the apartment I often felt uncomfortable in his company; now I felt sorry for him.

The long, drawn-out lunch was followed by an even longer dinner. In the brief intermezzo, I played a little with the children in the playground with the green dress pulled up to my thighs, which had become a little less scrawny (you would have said, You're putting on weight, M.). Until I spotted the father of the bride, who was standing silently under a locust tree that had lost its flowers, smoking a thin cigarette and watching me with unblinking eyes, his mouth ajar and rubbing his crotch with his other hand. Nobody stopped him; after all, the girl had been paid for.

GETTING ON TOWARD TEN o'clock, Philippe, the father, suddenly appeared before me. "Time for the children to go," he said, and that included me. He took the older kids in his car, I had to climb into a taxi with the four youngest. We drove through the dark park, then through a suburb, and then through the Bois de Boulogne. Coming from this side, Paris loomed up very suddenly, the trees sliding apart like a curtain the city was waiting behind.

I was relieved to see the buildings again. I had begun to recognize them as my point of reference, the place where everything always began and ended. We went to Philippe's parental home, the horseshoe-shaped apartment I would now enter through the front door for the first time, trailing nine sleepy, drooping children we needed to ferry up in two batches in the elevator. Philippe opened the front door without a word and led the way. He kept whispering, as if his mother might be somewhere around a corner. But the apartment was dark and empty, the shutters closed.

Two guest rooms had been prepared for the pale cousins. Without making a sound they stripped off their best clothes, hung them over the side of the bed, and crept in between sheets that felt cold, despite the warm weather. Nicolas and Louis would sleep in a room with me, a room that was half the size of their entire apartment.

I don't know what made it all so sorrowful. The total silence, the dejected children, the gloomy atmosphere? Knowing that my own bed was a few floors up and that I longed for it? Because of Philippe perhaps, who lingered awkwardly in the hall (his hall, but still, a stranger) before pressing some money into my hand ("For tomorrow morning. You'll find your own way in the kitchen. Everyone will be picked up around midday. Have a good evening")? Or the fact that I, when I finally went to bed, saw that the three of us were sleeping in what must have been Philippe's childhood bedroom?

12

ONE MORNING SOON AFTER the wedding, Philippe was still at home. An agitated conversation fell silent the moment I opened the door. I began quietly tidying up, the mood was overcast and we gave each other a wide berth, inasmuch as that was possible, *pardon, excusez-moi*. Finally Philippe left and Laurence sat down at the dining table, smoking and talking to her sister on the phone in mumbled, plaintive, abbreviated sentences. She didn't go to work, but still wanted me to stay and occupy myself with the children. I was relieved when it was time to put Louis—tiny, innocent Louis, who was still completely unsuspecting, of everything in the whole world—into the stroller to go and pick Nicolas up from school. He wasn't his usual self either and took my hand of his own accord. We passed the playground and kept walking, in tacit agreement that this was a day when it would be better to go farther.

On the bridge to Parc de l'Île Saint-Germain the dust of the passing cars blew in our faces. Louis screwed up his eyes as I pushed the wobbly-wheeled stroller along the walkway, which was separated from the road by a low concrete barrier. On the left, the faint silhouette of the Eiffel Tower was a pin pushed into the hazy sky, reduced to a construction of toothpicks in a city for tourists.

In the park we sought cover under the still-young trees; the large playing field had withered in the sun. The roar from the roads around this park, an island in the Seine, curved over the bowl-shaped field like a dome. On the short side, high on the edge, stood a . . . thing. I was too surprised to question it, but it was an object that didn't look like anything that was familiar to me.

A colored lump that was at least sixty feet high, it was painted with black lines and blue, red and gray surfaces: a brand-new, pre-historic totem. The thing seemed to have faces, vague features, eyes and noses, and open mouths that blurred the moment I tried to focus on them, like the man in the moon.

The boys and I stayed where we were for a while, sitting in the shade and chewing on the flattened baguette with melted chocolate in it, washing it down with water. The people around us were acting like there was nothing unusual about anything.

"Viens," said Nicolas. The shy boy, whose true self I had, in three months, only very occasionally glimpsed, started walking directly at whatever it was. I put Louis on my shoulders and followed him, his schoolbag and the folded stroller clasped under one arm.

Up close, the tower was bigger and coarser than from a distance, with lumpy protrusions a smooth surface had been drawn over. An abstract cartoon sprawled over the outside and into the indentations, like folded skin. Nicolas now entered through a tall, half-open door. I followed him with a grumbling Louis on my shoulders, his little hands grabbing at my short hair.

The inside was a whitewashed cavelike spiral, where every step, plateau, and bulge was marked with thick black lines. Directionless indirect light from above and below lit up the rough walls I ran my hand over, just like in Philippe's parental home a few weeks earlier. We climbed in silence, breathing in the musty, slightly chemical smell, not bad enough to put you off. There was nobody else there.

Nicolas ran ahead, jumping up the big, wide steps, knocking on the walls, disappearing out of sight for a moment, then reappearing again, but all without a word. The corridors widened and narrowed; I had to get little Louis down off my shoulders to pass through. I let him crawl and clamber ahead. We ascended through the cochlea, the brain, or maybe the bowels of this object, then lingered in an attic, disappointed that it had come to an end. After that we descended more slowly, disoriented by the lines around us and placing our feet carefully, as if drunk.

(Now, so many years later and with internet, I could tell you that we were in a tower by the artist Dubuffet, a work of art that had been opened shortly before. And that it would deteriorate in the years that followed until it was a moldy green ruin, that it would later be bought and restored. This installation was his most important structure, after all. I could color the event and dress it up with factoids. Would that matter? I now cherish that experience, free of foreknowledge, the kind of event that would later become less and less common and finally no longer happen at all.)

When we were outside again the children remained silent. Then Nicolas started to laugh and I followed his example, surrendering to whinnying giggles that spread through my body and into my knees. It was the discharge of a thunderstorm and I was certain that something indescribable had realigned itself. The children's hands fit better in mine, if nothing else.

THE OPPRESSIVE ATMOSPHERE IN the cramped apartment continued. No one discussed it with me, it was up to me to find a way to do my job and help the two children through the day. What they had to eat, who had to be picked up where and when, I figured it out myself. The time that Philippe returned from work began to vary. He arrived much earlier or much later than usual and went straight to the bedroom without turning on the TV or the Minitel. When I passed the bedroom carrying the washing basket or with my hands full of toys, he was sitting on the bed with his eyes closed. I could have spent the night in the corner next to the sofa, nobody would have noticed, but eventually, after his return, I would leave the building silently, feeling like I had left the boys out with the garbage. It was only on my way to the bus stop, walking through the twilight, that I started to recover my own form.

THE LAMBERTS HAD THEIR problems. All the people in all the Metros had their problems. The whole world had problems. The Cold War, that soundtrack of my childhood, would end. In Berlin the wall would fall but I still couldn't read the papers. There were strange new objects in the city; I would see more of them. I tried to build something up, no matter how futile, while a cold wind was still blowing through my previous life. What a mess. All these loose ends. I needed to resolve something, I had to once again worm my way through a network of corridors and the only tools I had were a jar of BIC ballpoints and a graph-paper notebook.

After visiting the Dubuffet with the children, I picked up the notebook and thought: Maybe I need to rid myself of our story—which had stopped six months before and now seemed to be receding, my history with you that seemed, in this new situation, more and more like fiction—maybe I needed to purge myself in one fell swoop.

So that's what I did. In a couple of evenings I wrote it all down. I recently typed those pages out on the laptop, about half a notebook, and of course I fiddled around with it. Editing. Changing things, tightening, deleting—you know better than anyone, Flo, what montage can do. What remains is the last version, that one that sets and is etched onto the plate, which I will now tell you.

III

Flo and M.

1987–1989

A COUPLE OF DAYS after the Duke (after I'd drunk the glass of beer you'd given me while my hair dried in the warm air of the bar; after you'd interrogated me with a few summary questions while leaning back on your stool; after you'd run your languid eyes up and down my body as if inspecting a calf at market), I find a card in my pigeonhole. It's a still from *Citizen Kane*, the famous one where Charles Foster Kane is addressing a crowd in front of an enormous picture of himself, his right arm outstretched in a gesture that takes in the whole world. You mentioned the film casually—"Come and polish up your knowledge of film if you like, there's a lot you have to see. *Kane*, start with *Citizen Kane*." Now I have an invitation in your determined capitals.

OPEN HOUSE AT MY PLACE EVERY FRIDAY. COME SOMETIME. FLO.

Again, I get the feeling there's a spotlight trained on me as I stand with the card in my hand in the cramped hall of the house I share with other students. It's a Thursday. Going the next day would seem desperate. I wait a week.

THE ADDRESS IS CLOSE by, I know the street. A street along a canal that makes you think, If I could live here my life would begin. Since moving to the city, I've ridden my bike along it sometimes on my way somewhere else, always feeling I needed an excuse to be there. Art Deco stained glass above tall front doors, high-ceilinged rooms, and front yards that have been neglected with stylish nonchalance. Classic cars parked out front.

It's number 42, one of the set-back buildings halfway along the quay. All of the windows, on every floor, are lit up. First I stand at the gate for a while with my back to the dark water of the canal. The door is ajar despite the wintry cold and I can hear loud music, a symphony orchestra at full volume. I grip the gate, its metal ice-cold on my hand. There's a bottle of supermarket wine in my bag and I think, I could just get back on my bike and go home.

The front door is thrown open by a falling, stumbling body. A young shaven-headed guy in a leather coat, tartan pants held together with safety pins. He rolls down the steps, scrambles to his feet, and backs off a little. I recognize him as a third-year, maybe. There are a few different guys who still hold true to punk and I never dare to look any of them straight in the eye. A man who could pass for a bouncer appears in the doorway—Robbie. The orchestral music floods out with him (Mussorgsky's "Baba Yaga"? I'm not sure, Flo, but it's plausible). The bedraggled punk's role is apparently over; he disappears with his tail between his legs. The brawny man beckons me, because of the sawing violins I can't tell if he's saying something too. He gestures again, Come in, hurry up a bit. And I do.

I'VE BEEN LIVING IN D. for a couple of months now. It's not that I never go to parties, never seek out company. I do, but everything is provisional. My fellow students and I are each other's "for want of better." People to fill gaps with, practice people. We snuffle around each other and all know that this is not yet it. We're seventeen, eighteen, nineteen, not yet solidified, pressed out of the molds of our respective families and now, without that structure, without that fixed form, it's like we've started spreading. We're all desperately looking for a life that suits us. A character, an image, a style, a goal perhaps, or at least a typical characteristic or striking way of speaking. None of us can wait to take those first steps and at the same time we're all equally terrified.

Where do we start? How do you do it? The first time I go to eat at a fellow student's, the puff pastry quiche from the supermarket recipe is followed by us going to bed together on his mattress on pallets on the floor. Is it out of surprise that a boy, or is he already a man, has cooked for me that I think that one must lead to the other? That this is what adults do—not sneakily in a park behind school or in the apartment building's bicycle room, but simply in a bed after a dinner? He goes to work on me hastily and with his head turned. I remember a rice-paper lampshade and a green alarm clock and the hope that arousal would arrive, or something pleasant, but it chafes, it hurts, then it's over and he says, while rolling a cigarette, Nice, huh?

That night, the first of many in your house on the canal, it occurred to me for the first time that I might not have to invent everything myself, that it might also be possible to just enter a new phase. Simply by going in through a front door.

SOMEBODY HAS PUT ON Sun Ra. Picturing the rooms now, with books from the floor to the ceiling and randomly placed furniture, the image coincides with the jittery drums, the lowest registers on the piano, and a floating flute. We students play Duran Duran, the Cure, maybe Prince, interesting seniors listen to David Sylvian—how childish that suddenly seems.

You walk up in a green velvet dress that sweeps the floor, glass of wine in one hand, and with the other you gently squeeze my shoulder. "Good that you've come. I knew you would." Your expansive curls almost fold your narrow face inward. You turn to the scattered company, eight or nine people who are all at least ten years older than me. Nobody is sitting in or on a chair, they're hanging around as if on a film set, decorating the enormous chesterfield in the middle of the room, or lying stretched out on each other's laps. Robbie is leaning with one buttock on a big marble dining table—all of the furniture in your house is large and heavy and immovable. A hunting rifle is lying on the table as a decoration; a film prop, you tell me later. Two women are sprawled on the rug in front of the burning fire. Sisters who both have the same wide-set eyes. They look up at me like disturbed cats.

"People, this is Marie. She's going to be a photographer, so watch out. Marie, these are . . . the people," you say. It is the first time that someone has named my future profession out loud, as if the decision has suddenly been made. For myself, I'm not so sure.

You pour me a glass of wine, the action so smooth and effortless, and put me down on a chair next to a coffee table with a large book of photos on it, a luxury edition with the photographs of Horst P. Horst. "Just got it, have a look," you say—how easily you resolve my insecurity, giving me something to do, a role in this new theater. I stay for an hour or two, not much longer, and riding my bike home, I think, Now, now at last.

⌒

YOU DO A THOROUGH job of it. After my introduction to your circle, a book is delivered to my house. A card with the film poster from *A Clockwork Orange* is with it, a film I haven't seen yet. Again those capitals. "I'LL LEND YOU A BOOK NOW AND THEN. COME AND SWAP IT WHEN YOU'RE DONE WITH IT, FLO." The large white plastic bag contains a large, white, square, floppy book wrapped in tissue paper.

I wipe the table in the shared kitchen clean, lay the book on it, and open it at random. Two naked women with daggers at their hips and ropes constricting their fat bodies turn their blindfolded faces toward me.

I close the book again and sit for a moment. Then open it to the same page. Yes, I see it. I leaf past more trussed, deviant bodies: a pregnant woman whose belly is being carried by a dwarf, gaunt youths with antlers on their heads. Masculine women, feminine men wearing helmets, breasts with nipples as big as omelets, everything covered with sticky angel's hair. Black-and-white photos, magnificent prints, each scene lit before a dark, cloudy background, a torture chamber painted by Rembrandt (later I learn what that is, "Rembrandtesque").

I think this is your idea: for me not to know what I'm seeing, even if I *know* what I'm seeing.

This book has been discussed at school. A young photographer, Erwin Olaf, has depicted chess pieces in staged tableaux. It's somewhere between S-M and theater, they say—but nobody has a copy. Whatever else, this is completely different from the grainy reportage photos in *Vrij Nederland*, our inspiration at the time. And now that I've suddenly got it in my kitchen, it feels select and illicit. I hope nobody comes in, or that they do.

THE BOOKS KEEP COMING. Often they're new, sometimes already worn, and they drop into the letter box faster than I can return them. After Olaf comes *Sentimental Journey* by the Japanese photographer Nobuyoshi Araki: straightforward shots, mostly of his wife. Sometimes naked, sometimes with just her childlike upper body exposed. Lying on a lawn in jeans, sitting in a room next to a suit of armor—besides all the alienation, a word I constantly hear from our instructors, I mainly see her expressionless eyes, her impassive face. Her surrender to him—her husband, her photographer—is that the essence? The essence of love? The books don't come with instructions, you don't tell me what to make of them. I have to look.

As a contrast—*I think, I don't know your plan*—it's followed by Jean-Paul Goude's *Jungle Fever*, with a caged Grace Jones on the cover. Loud colors, photomontage, black women, black men looking more like sculptures than people. Helmut Newton drops into the letter box, more naked women, white women this time, bored rich women waiting for sex with their butler or tennis coach.

Ed van der Elsken, an original Dutch edition of *Love on the Left Bank*: "The actions in this book and the characters that play a role in them are products of the author's imagination." I copy the sentence out in my pocket calendar. The "author" surprises me; it's the photographer, who can apparently also be an author, someone who can make things up. Everything is new.

You're careless with your books. This book, this magnificent book is battered and thumbed. Some of the pages are torn, it's as worn and weary as the bars and people in the photos. I look at a Paris that no longer exists. A city in black and white, with heavily lined eyes looking into tarnished mirrors. That's how you want to live, but also not at all, I think. They're always short of money and always cold, but so beautiful.

With Cindy Sherman, your photo therapy starts to take effect. I love it the moment I open it. This book, I want to keep. She has a face that in itself doesn't express anything specific and she is merciless in the way she uses that blank face. Her *Untitled Film Stills* imprint themselves on my memory. Number 10: A woman squats on the kitchen floor to pick up the contents of her torn shopping bag and looks up as if she's about to be hit by a man who's not in the photo at all—how can you cram so much foreboding into one image? And how can it be the same woman as number 53, the housewife in a starched top, ashamed, humiliated, next to a floor lamp? They're archetypes, I read later, but I have never seen them like this before. How can someone come up with this, make it, and also be all of it herself?

. . .

I SHOULD ASK MYSELF why this is happening to me, whether other students get books from you as well, why this preferential treatment. But I don't. I choose not to. As a result I could think, Everything that comes next is my own fault. I haven't taken any of your classes yet, maybe you just like to share your knowledge. Maybe it's just nice of you. Why shouldn't that be one of the possibilities?

⌒

ON FRIDAY EVENINGS I can now be found installed in a wing chair in a corner of your living room, in your large, deep house on the canal. Nobody asks me any questions, I don't have to put on music or tell jokes or supply booze. I'm plied with wine or beer or vodka or tea in flavors I, raised on store-brand tea bags, have never heard of. They're kept in large tins in a slide-out pantry in the high-ceilinged kitchen. Lemon verbena, Lapsang souchong, hibiscus. Sometimes it's busy in the house, sometimes there are just a few people, but you're never alone on a Friday evening. Robbie is always there. A short, taciturn man with a wide, flat head and vaguely Asian features, he rents your attic and you refer to him in turn as your tenant, good friend, bouncer, cook, and assistant— none of these designations seem to please him more than the others. On Friday evenings he's at the front door or in the kitchen, where he grinds large amounts of chili in a mortar to make the sambal he spreads on everything he eats.

Nobody, except for you now and then, pays any particular attention to me, but that simplifies things. I'm like a plant that's been put in a corner and is being given time to acclimatize.

THERE ARE BOOKS TO read and look at, record covers to study, a whole pile of old *Interview Magazines* I leaf through with great awe—Andy Warhol died at the start of the year. It feels like I missed a boat you and your friends take regularly. You talk about Warhol as if he too could come through the door at any moment, Andy will this and Andy will that and the Factory is like this or that. It seems there's a new Warhol too: He's called Jeff Koons and he's made glass tanks in which basketballs float weightlessly, and a life jacket executed in bronze. Opinions about him vary, especially when the booze is flowing, and that's always. Can he or can he not fill Andy's shoes? Is there anything to it, is it brilliant Post-Pop or simple theft, is Koons just the latest wannabe, or is he unique? He started off as a stockbroker, that's the kind of thing you know, and the discussion keeps coming back to it. Is it possible to go from that to art? Or is it the perfect preparation? These questions seem important.

I keep my mouth shut and let the *Interview* pages slip through my fingers. They're big and flimsy with glaring, full-bleed photos of glittering people who look like they're made of plastic. Grace Jones has a thousand pairs of shoes she keeps in boxes on which she's stuck Polaroids of each pair. She always flies wearing a couple of furs, one over the other, because she won't have them in the hold, and she gives her mother a fur every year as a gift. She considers questions as to whether she is a man or a woman passé. "The future is no sex."

IN THE CORNER WITH my chair, which has simply become "my" chair, is a large glass display case with objects that would have been seen as old rubbish in the apartment building I grew up in. Here they acquire an indisputable aura.

Wineglasses with a stem but not a foot, in a vase like a bunch of flowers. A whole collection of thumbed Baedeker travel guides. An armadillo handbag. Russian hammer-and-sickle vodka glasses. More hammer-and-sickles: on pins, caps, little flags, a biscuit tin. A few unopened bottles of wine with animal labels—a hare, a rabbit, an elephant, a flamingo. A nineteenth-century iron and an iron that looks like an American car. Tortoiseshell combs. Fluorescent wristbands. Real cans of Campbell's soup (tomato, of course, but also chicken noodle and cream of mushroom). Shells as big as a child's head. Tennis balls in six fluorescent colors. Rodin's *Thinker*, in plaster, four inches tall.

There is no connection between anything. Did you find it all, are they gifts, do these things have emotional value? There are oil portraits Robbie buys at flea markets, never altogether successful: people with unintentionally crossed eyes or hair that looks like a dollop of dirty whipped cream. He also collects embroidered old Dutch sayings: "East west, home's best," or a picture of a clockface and the line "This dial shows your dying hour." Further: old Simenon paperbacks; statues of the Virgin Mary with lamps in them; a Virgin with a thermometer in it; a Virgin whose cloak you can open to reveal her naked Betty Boop boobs; bits of torn advertising posters arranged by color (a whole shelf full, sometimes someone changes the composition); "Und so fort, und so weiter," as one of your friends always says before braying with laughter, and so on and so forth, I've forgotten his name. At the Documenta in Kassel he recently pulled a double all-nighter with the Dutch artist Rob Scholte, he says. The anecdote lends him authority.

IT WAS ONLY LATER that it became clear to me that this was no Wunderkammer, not a collection of curiosities, objects that have been gathered here because each has its own unique character and beauty, value and peculiarity. That is *so* nineteenth century, it couldn't possibly be that. No, this is a postmodern, *ironic* collection. The admiration for these objects, discussing them, adding to them, and sometimes replacing them is the essence of the display case—not the objects themselves. Nothing can be taken at face value, the things are just vehicles. They stand for something else. They are unintentionally beautiful or unintentionally ugly. And you and your friends understand that. Or rather, you decide it, you know what can be ironically collected or admired, eaten or drunk, put on and worn. Through the intention of things, you see their real character.

Where do you get this knowledge? I sit in the corner and try to crack the code.

The first time I dare to ask something, I've already got it wrong. In the case there is also a shelf with framed family photos, at least twenty, carefully arranged in a gentle arc according to increasing and then decreasing size. Poor quality, they all have the strange orange cast of cheap prints. When I ask who the people are, all those faces with no clear resemblance, you let out a snort of laughter that makes me immediately regret my question. You then address me with my full first name. "They're discards, Marie. I find them at flea markets, boxes full of them. Everybody's constantly taking photos of each other and sticking them in albums."

You pick one out of the row and hold it at an angle so we can both see it: a solidly built woman in a tight miniskirt pushing a baby carriage. A housing development in construction stretches out behind her, the road still sand with tire tracks between newly laid sidewalks.

"It seems so important, recording your life like that. Birth, vacation, amusement parks, the first baby, the first car. Leaning toward a cake each birthday and blowing out the candles. And everyone follows that same well-trodden path, all those albums share a single pattern. I bet I could find the same scenes at your parents'."

I DON'T SAY A word. I think of the three albums with glassine interleaves on the lowest shelf of the wobbly bookcase in the hall at home. We don't have many photos and yes, they're the same pictures as these ones here: a wedding, a photo of the empty, just-finished apartment. The first crib with me in it, second daughter in the same crib, third daughter. The Toyota Corolla with my parents posing in front of it, my father's hair already thinning.

You sit down on the arm of the large chair. Your leather pants on that red velvet feel warm and familiar. I think, This must be what it's like to have a big sister who knows the world.

"When the people in them die, these photos are suddenly"—you tap the glass of the frame—"nothing. Then a distant cousin shows up who doesn't dare to throw them in the trash or burn them, so they put them in a box for the charity store. Out of sight. Maybe an artist can do something with them." You run your finger over the glass and put the photo back. "People who get rid of their family—what do you think, is that sad?"

You look at me and I don't know what to say in reply. At that time my own family is something I mainly try to ignore. I haven't visited my parents for weeks.

"You can also see it as liberating," you answer yourself. You screw up your eyes and pull my cigarette—something I've just learned to cling to—from between my fingers and stub it out in the pot of a large monstera. "You have to quit, you know," you say, bringing your face up close. "It makes you ugly."

⌐

EARLY IN THE NEW Year, you appear at my place. The doorbell rings (3x for Marie), I walk to the door in my sweats; it's still early.

It's a pale Saturday morning and I'm working on an assignment. We've taken photos "with shadows and/or graphic patterns" and have to make a collage from the prints. Maybe it's around this time that I've started having doubts about carrying on with the course, a feeling I will never express to you, the one person who's gone to so much trouble on my behalf. You've opened a door for me, backing out now would be ungrateful.

But the assignments feel like homework and I just want to get them out of the way. My desk is covered with torn and cut-up photos of paving stones, countertops, a knitted sweater, bicycle racks, stacks of cheap clothes at Zeeman. I'm still not used to taking photos; in my hands the camera feels large and ostentatious. They're all quick and timid snaps, taken randomly with neither taste nor preference, as long as it's a pattern. We get our assessments later this month and I'm dreading it. The creative talent a teacher foisted on me one afternoon in high school seems very far away. Your gray Citroën CX is parked at the curb and you're leaning on it and waiting. "I thought I'd drop by," you say, your eyes colored by sunglasses with square green lenses. "See where I'm actually sending those books." Arms crossed, you look down the street, where red paper mush from the New Year's fireworks still cakes the gutters. "Here, apparently."

You push yourself off the car and step over to my front door, the taps under your boots clicking on the sidewalk.

"Get dressed, we're going on an outing. I'll wait in your kitchen."

My kitchen . . . my kitchen is filthy, there are encrusted cereal bowls on top of yesterday's dirty dishes, the day before yesterday's, and some that are even older. My three housemates and I do everything separately and as a result everything gets out of hand. I only really get on with Daniel, a sixth-year econometrics student. Sometimes we do a bit of cleaning together.

The countertop is beyond salvation. I offer you one of the four Formica chairs, quickly wipe the spatters off the coffee maker, and put on half a pot of coffee. You sit in the dirty kitchen like a queen. Completely at ease, as you seem to be everywhere. It's an image I cherish, Flo: the way a sudden sunbeam shines into the kitchen and sets your hair on fire and how all of a sudden it doesn't look like a dirty students' kitchen anymore. You drink your coffee black and say, "Just right." I go and get changed.

FIRST WE "GO FOR a drive." At home, at my former home, that's not something they'd start the Corolla for, they always need a destination first. We're driving just to drive, you say. You're driving, I'm sitting next to you. It's cold, the asphalt roads have frozen to a pale gray, and a haze of minuscule glitter is hanging in the sky. The car is humming, a warm cocoon of stationary air, music, and curiosity.

You have a steady stream of questions for me, and expect real answers. Where do I come in my family? What does my room at home look like? Which image has stuck with me? Do I like sweet or savory? Which film, which book, what kind of music? Can I remember a decisive moment in high school? What did my friends eat, drink, smoke? Am I in love? What's my favorite word? Do I like dancing? Where do I want to go?

I watch the road and the answers come of their own accord, even emerging more beautifully than usual. I make up some extra friends, I pad out my first assignments a little, mention films and books I only know the titles of. It's not difficult to lie, the version I'd like to be comes out very naturally. I suspect you see through it all, but if so, you keep it to yourself. We stop for lunch somewhere, another extravagance that suddenly feels very natural. You send your toasted ham-and-cheese sandwich back because it's not hot enough and accept a new one without looking at the waitress.

THE ROAD NORTH IS long, you're taking me to the edge of the country. A knot of houses is wedged between the dunes and the dike, and beyond that is the great nothing. We stop at a parking lot next to a hamburger joint at the foot of the lighthouse. You shut the car door but don't lock it, you never do. Ahead of me, you climb the stairs up the dike with long strides, two steps at a time. The morning sun has vanished. Above the protection of the concrete breakwater a strong wind blasts our faces. Floating in the air like kites, seagulls exchange shrill screeches as they hold their positions. Wet gusts hit our cheeks. You're peering at an island in the distance, or is it a sandbank, and when you turn back there's a red glow on your face. For the first time, I see that you have blood flowing through your veins. I wonder if you might be in love with me, a thought so arrogant I immediately nip it off.

We walk along the curved dike for a while, the vague island unmoving on the otherwise empty horizon. You take some photos. I don't pay attention to what you're photographing, but carefully watch how you do it. In your hands the camera seems like a natural object, an extension of your body. Focusing and clicking is second nature to you, like tying a sash. That's how casual it has to be, I think. If I can't manage that, I have to give it up. This is how you should want to take pictures, just fishing them up out of the stream. Later, when we're warming up again in the car, I want to take back everything I exaggerated on the way here, but I don't know where to start. You play a cassette, David Byrne, and hum along, your slender fingers tapping the wheel. By the time the city comes into view it's already dark. We've struck up another conversation after all and turn in to the streets still talking. I don't know how we got onto the subject, but by the time you've dropped me off at my place, I've agreed to a portrait photograph.

"We'll do it after your first assessment," you say.

As your red taillights turn out of my street, I go inside thinking that this has been the most amazing day of my life.

⌒

OF COURSE, I COULD have gone to the library to see what kind of work you make. I could have found *Het boek Saul* (1983) and

Dagen met Doreen (1985), the two series of photographs that had made you reasonably well known. I could have seen how you followed the Antwerp rabbi Saul, capturing his daily transformation from an ordinary man into a religious leader and back again. Classic photo reportage, but from extremely close by—even into Saul's beard, his big ears, his wrinkled hands with their strange large nails, his worn suit. Brazen on your part and daring of Saul. Sitting at the table among family members, he radiates authority. But in the run-down streets of Antwerp, from behind in full daylight, you show him as a shady scrap metal merchant children looked away from in fright.

The book was met with high praise and indignant protest (it was either unadorned truth or antisemitism in a new guise) but you didn't respond; the pictures spoke for themselves. Your name was remembered.

And then Doreen, the wife of a US soldier stationed in West Germany, in Heidelberg. A hard American beauty with a slight squint, photographed between the white buildings of the enormous American compound. Doreen too had evidently let you shadow her for weeks, months on end. On the first pages, her life seems so fresh and organized and cheerful, but the repetition (school, tea parties, visiting the hairdressing salon, doing the shopping in the cutesy little town, her crew-cut husband, the roast chickens) soon becomes as suffocating as a slowly tightening noose. This book was translated into English and the series *Days with Doreen* enjoyed a modest museum tour of Germany and the Netherlands. There were also four photos included in the "Daily Life" section of the 1986 World Press Photo exhibition, an achievement none of our other instructors can lay claim to.

BUT THAT'S SOMETHING I don't do. I don't go to the library. I don't even look in your bookcase, where a short row of your own books are on the shelf: Florence da Silva, between Salgado and Stieglitz. I see all of that much later. It simply doesn't occur to me and besides, if I had seen them, I would have probably been just as flattered by your attention. Maybe even more so.

⁓

THE FIRST ASSESSMENT HAS taken the form of a scene from *The Singing Detective*, a TV series that showed recently and enjoys a certain cult status, with videos going from hand to hand among the students. (But you shouldn't gush about it too much, you'd do better to watch the films of Tarkovsky or Fassbinder's *Berlin Alexanderplatz*.)

In the series, a detective has been hospitalized with severe psoriasis—his face is a flaking mask of yellowish-pink skin. In the delusions brought on by the disease and the drugs he's taking, doctors and nurses slide into view, pull the curtain around his bed, interrogate him without waiting for his answers, and burst into spontaneous song and dance.

Just like that patient, we, the foundation-year students, wait next to a display of our work for the visitation. Our work is still so cautious. Collages, material studies, badly printed photos, first attempts at something conceptual. It's all flakes and peeling skin and so are we. After lunch, which is also an extended discussion, the committee sweeps back into the classroom en bloc, faces red from the wine they've been drinking. The instructors are more long-winded than in their classes, they've turned up the volume too, puffing up their chests for their colleagues.

"Marie, here, yeah . . ." says my supervisor, a graphic designer, male with a goatee and an abruptly bulging gut above his corduroy waistband. "I think it still needs some work. Looking at this portfolio, there is a . . . sensitivity for structures." He picks one of my collages up by the corner like a dirty dishcloth and lets it dangle in the air for a moment. "But I would say, in terms of content, it's only just scraping the surface."

The other instructors now start zealously rooting through the presentation, putting everything back the wrong way round or passing it on to someone else. In the first semester we're not expected to respond, that's only from the second semester on. The instructors say all kinds of things to each other. The word *expressiveness* comes up a few times, and *urgency*. As in, that's what's lacking.

The students who had their assessment in the morning have come back in with the instructors, relieved or intent on vengeance as if they've just been hazed. You can smell them. Twenty-five strong in a ring around the instructors and me. More than anything else, what I need in this moment is a hole to sink into.

"What I notice, Marie," says our perspective instructor—who comes from Groningen and has been making us draw and photograph the same arrangement of plates and vases on a velvet cloth since September according to the motto "It's not the motif but the approach that matters"—"is that you . . . I notice that you hardly dewjhdikklo lkkncipoc cn;r;yi;a, and then soim, olsh, hashaowyf, just ns; oidf, jrhfydkfuyj dkhli oiuddh xc and qcfdgstl, yeah?"

I look at him and see the fluorescent tubes above his head throbbing. "I'm not sure I've understood you properly," I say. His yellowish eyes stab into me.

"Have I not made myself clear?" He looks around, the others raise their eyebrows, shake their heads. No, no, he's been perfectly clear.

"Am I speaking Greek?" Laughter.

"What I mean is you bnxcvkso hdn and oifdvn, jdfioscmmx to spoc skjd, ncjdiks ht woiskdco, so that kjfoimck jenoskm."

In the background the other students start to blur, turning into rings of sweaters, shoes, bags, and hair colors, rotating at different speeds. I see my little portraits lying in the middle and wish they would crumble and be carried off by a gust of wind.

The instructor drops a few more phrases, scattering them around and over me, but I only catch the word *mediocrity*, pronounced with a wet northern *t*. He rounds off. A student in the group of listeners is called on to provide commentary, just as with all the previous candidates. The instructors make sure these students have already had their own assessment, so they "feel free to speak." If the staff members have been critical, the student generally twists the knife; if they have praised the work, he or she starts gushing nervously. The philosophy and society professor—who embraces each new year as an opportunity to once again go on and on about the Milgram experiment—came up with this system.

I know the guy she has selected, I actually know him reasonably well. At the start of the year we took turns with three others to cook for each other. It petered out fairly quickly because he thought our standards weren't up to scratch, not rising above tortillas and macaroni and cheese; his expectations had been higher. He's the only snob in the whole course, the first person in my life with his own wine rack. He has red patches on his cheeks and full wet lips he plants everywhere and nowhere after dinners. This morning the committee trashed his photos.

"It's all, um . . . rather small," he says. "Rather small-minded, I mean. I just find it difficult to grasp what Marie is trying to say. Or if she's trying to say anything at all."

I see his face as through a magnifying glass, with black craters and fleshy nostrils, his wide neck disappearing into his tennis shirt.

"Maybe it's a question of the frame of reference," he continues. "That more needs to be put into it, before it can come out, if you see what I mean." Heads nod approvingly. Maybe on closer consideration his photos aren't that bad after all, you see them thinking. The drawings and photos I'm quite satisfied about—because they exist too, I mustn't forget that—have somehow all ended up at the bottom of the chaotic pile on the table.

I pass, *just*, though my head was on the chopping block. Nothing stays with me from the commentary, only the bottomless feeling that everyone is right. I have a clear image of the classroom door opening somewhere toward the end and you slipping in. You listen at a distance, your long, brick-red sweater glowing in the corner of my eye like a flag. You're gazing past me and out the window. The next moment clothes and paper and feet rustle as the caravan moves on and everyone disappears, you too, without a trace.

ACROSS FROM THE HOUSE I'm living in is a building that once served as a chocolate factory but now contains a few workshops and studios—in a distant future, if I can get some kind, any kind of practice off the ground, maybe I'll be able to rent something there. Not long after the assessment, I spot Robbie parking in the street and going inside; shortly after that, again. One day he's coming out as I approach. It's awkward bumping into each other in this location; hesitantly I raise a hand. I see Robbie mostly as part of the furniture at your place and, as I mentioned, we rarely speak. Here in my street he looks even stockier, wider than he is tall. He greets me casually, as if nothing could be more ordinary, and gets into your car. When I ask you about it, you say that he's rented a small workplace where he's doing some experiments on a new printing process for you.

"I don't want those chemicals in the house, this is much more practical. He's good at stuff like that," you say. It sounds logical. You have a practice, an assistant, projects you can't talk about just yet because that disturbs the creative process—I hear things like that all the time from you, the other instructors, the people at your house, everyone who has the knowledge I am still searching for.

YOU DO THE PORTRAIT at your house in a north-facing room at the front on the second floor. The room is not very deep, but wide and high-ceilinged, and you only occasionally use it as a studio—you take most of your photos on location. The windows are covered with dark foil up to eye height so that the indirect light floats down from above. The walls are white—one has a gray curtain you can draw across it—and there are a couple of Persian carpets on the bare floorboards to keep out the cold. Your plate camera is set up next to an empty fireplace and I have to pose in front of it, sitting on a low barstool.

"North light is softer. Not colder, as people think, but veiled. It doesn't come from a single source, there are no shadows." You look down at the ground glass. "It comes from everywhere and nowhere at once, creeping into all the nooks and crannies . . ." Looking at me, looking down again. "Making people more beautiful. More vulnerable, but more beautiful."

You asked me to put on a white blouse, but rejected the one I was wearing when I arrived. With my back turned, I pull on the shirt you've given me. It's the first time I'm going to be looked at so officially, through a camera. There's nothing beautiful about me, nothing worth seeing—there wasn't before and there still isn't. North light can't change that. Still, I agreed to be photographed and now I'm here and it feels like I'm standing on a chair in the middle of a crowded room.

I try to banish the assessment from two weeks ago from my thoughts, not daring to bring it up. I wonder if I really did see you there, if it wasn't just my imagination. I try to concentrate on the cracks in the plaster. You're sunny and chatting away.

"You know, Marie, I see . . ." Looking down, at me, down again. "That you've got good bone structure. Cheekbones, clavicles, shoulder bones, all in the right place. But . . ." You walk over to me, take hold of my shoulders as if gripping a box, turn me slightly to the light, walk back. "I think you still have to lose a little puppy fat. The structure is hidden." You walk back over to me, grab me by the shoulders again, and squeeze gently, as if to let me feel the bones. Then you press my cheekbones with your fingers, softly, as if shaping them, and then the corners of my jaw, my chin. I stare into space while you're touching my face; your hands smell of luxury. Although it doesn't take long, it lasts for a long time, then you let go.

You set to work with the light meter, walking toward and away from me with it in your hand, reading it out.

"Hm."

You take a Polaroid, put it aside, lower a shade on one of the windows, stare at the ground glass, put the shade back up. Study the Polaroid, say "hm" again. Outside the world is gray, on standby. The trees in front of your house, of which I can only see the tops, sketch a bare unmoving pattern in the mist. Water murmurs in the pipes, the sound suggesting warmth. I try to block out the cold. Puppy fat. You slide a film holder into the camera, pull out the dark slide.

"Can you raise your chin a little . . . no, not too much. Look at me. Good. No. Look back down again. Look at the corner of the window, the border between inside and outside. Yes, lovely." You press the button. Push the slide back in, pull out the holder. Pick up the tripod and move the camera seven or eight inches closer. The measuring starts again from the beginning.

"So that's something you could work on. I'm not saying you have to, but you could. A healthier diet, perhaps, or one that's not quite as unhealthy. I don't know what goes on in that shared house of yours. . . . It's not hard to get your body under control, Marie, it's actually easy." The tripod slides a fraction closer. "You just have to . . . commit."

I sit there and no longer feel the cold, the embarrassment about my puppy fat is keeping me warm. I feel the bones inside me all the more. Cheekbone, clavicle, shoulder bones. *Your head bone's connected to your neck bone, your neck bone's connected to your backbone, your backbone's connected to your hip bone* . . . There's the soundtrack of *The Singing Detective*, rattling down the bones, wrapped in a superfluous layer. A layer I can shed. I've never seen myself like this before, but you, with your infallible eye, are undoubtedly right. There must be a better version hidden inside me.

It's also the afternoon you suggest, no, inform me, that from now on you won't refer to me as Marie, but as M. That's more adult, you say, less generic. "What's more, *M* is a beautiful letter. You're on the corners of all the world's cities." I told you, You're in a sunny mood.

It's exactly what I need at that moment. An improved body, a new name. It's possible.

YOU TAKE TEN OR so photos, the whole thing is done in less than three quarters of an hour. Then you don't mention it for weeks. The session doesn't seem to have taken place and I don't dare bring it up. Just when I'm about to leave after a Friday evening at your house, you let me see the result. In the hall you pull a print out of an envelope, hold it at an angle in front of me, studying it yourself too, as if it's somebody else's work.

It's a thoughtful portrait. I'm looking out through the window in what must be the third or fourth shot of the session. A light like Vermeer's—I now know what that means—falls through the window to my left, I'm three-quarters turned with only my torso and face visible. The borrowed white shirt is on the large side and hangs loosely on my body, foreshadowing the new, thinner version of myself I can become.

It's a classic portrait, not particularly striking or expressive, and I could have known, should have known, that this wasn't the photo you were looking for, not the photo you were going to use. I say it's beautiful, of course I do, you put it back in the envelope and hand it over as if passing me a newspaper. "The best thing about a photo is that it never changes, even when the people in it do," you say. Much, much later, I read that that's something Andy Warhol said.

I never see the photo again. At home I leave the envelope unopened behind my bed and later, when I'm leaving, it goes into the garbage container along with the rest. Now I regret that. I don't and will never know who it depicted.

THE LEAD-IN TO SUMMER is a period without signposting, unstructured and uninterrupted. Things start rolling, that's what it feels like. I produce work, it's acceptable, it even gets better. The theory classes are no longer an enormous gray area of ignorance and incomprehension. With a dictionary by my side, I plow through the writing of Michel Foucault and Jean Baudrillard, who both use words I never heard at home and will never say out loud. I give up my resistance to obscure and bombastic language and try to read on and discern the meaning. Sometimes I succeed.

I stick a new note next to the doorbell, "3x for M." My fellow students aren't bothered by my new name, we're more than halfway through the first year and others too have started tinkering with their identity. Bleaching their hair, painting their bikes, experimenting with eye shadow and drugs and objects they can insert in piercings. We shed our skins like snakes; I fail to notice that the new skins everyone pulls on are almost identical.

I lose weight, yes. As you predicted, it's not difficult. I start by eating a quarter less, then half as much. I avoid my housemates' pasta and chili sessions as much as possible, living mainly off oranges and lemons I buy in large quantities at the Alhambra supermarket; the acidity makes your stomach contract.

I start photographing my meals, the first project that is met with enthusiasm at school. I stand on a kitchen chair and photograph my carefully arranged plates (containing a single cracker, or an orange with its segments spread like a sun wheel, or a bowl of clear broth with nothing in it, or an egg out of the egg slicer) from directly above, in the middle of the frame and surrounded by the mess on the grimy kitchen table. The plates are immaculate islands in a sea of old newspapers, crumbs, dirty glasses, stained breadboards.

Looking at them, the photography instructor is surprised by this "development" and starts talking about Bernd and Hilla Becher and their classification of German industrial buildings, all photographed in black and white from directly in front, preferably in the dullest of weather conditions—I fetch their book *Typologies* from your bookcase. You ask me why, I say which instructor suggested it to me, whereupon you sniff scornfully and make minced meat of his recommendation. The myopia of it. My work has nothing to do with that; instead I'm trying to distill my personality from my daily activities, that's your take on it. You pull out a thin book from the 1960s by the artist Daniel Spoerri and show me how he glued the remnants of meals to the tops of tables and mapped them.

I'm honored. For the first time someone, you, no less, has bothered to analyze what I'm doing—and now I too find the instructor's Becher comparison naive. You study my photos carefully and at length, praising the fact that everything is so central. "You couldn't care less about the golden section, M.," you say. "That shows character. It's bold."

In February I still weigh 143 pounds, in April it's 128, by summer the scales are just nudging 110. It's gratifying to pull my belts a notch tighter, then another. I feel light and fit and ignore the remarks of my fellow students, who are all thin themselves, so what are they moaning about? What counts is you complimenting me. It suits me. How persistent of me. I look more mature. My eyes are bigger. See, those cheekbones! Have I ever considered bangs? Robbie can do it for me, he's really good at that too.

When I, very occasionally, go home for a visit, my mother is worried. My father says I look "scraggy." I resolve to stick it out. You could say that my self-confidence is growing per pound I lose. You could also say that I'm surrendering myself one pound at a time. I think, when it comes down to it, both are true.

MORE AND MORE OFTEN the phone rings late at night. You want to know if I'm studying, what I had for dinner, who I've seen. What am I reading? Do I understand it? Tell me. I'm standing in the hall of my shared house with the receiver to my ear and the telephone cord in my hand—later I put a stool there. Talking over the phone seems easier than face-to-face at your place, where the few comments I make are trumped by your friends, people of a different category. They're older, they do interesting things: set dressing, reportage. The "Und so fort, und so weiter" guy (Erick with ck, now I remember, when he's drunk he wants to stroke your hair and sometimes you let him, as if tossing a coin to a beggar) writes columns for the local rag under a pseudonym.

Or else they say they're artists with a "McJob"; it takes a while for me to figure out that doesn't mean they're flipping burgers. The petty job with no substance is a choice, and therefore heroic. It's how they liberate themselves from the pressure to achieve so they can "dedicate themselves to free work." They see me as a prop, I think, clearly a lightweight.

"They don't matter, M.," you say. "They come and go. They're a pleasant way to pass the time, I wouldn't call it friendship." You don't express an opinion whether what's developed between you and me *is* a friendship and I don't ask.

Because of the shared telephone at my house you tell me that you will let it ring briefly once and then call again. I start counting on those calls, postponing sleep until we've had our talk and feeling abandoned when the telephone stays quiet. You yourself don't say much during these conversations. You ask about my day and press me for details, eliciting endless descriptions of what I've been doing, who I've spoken to. I regularly make something up, not enough happens otherwise. Daniel is the only one who sometimes says something about it: What does somebody who calls that often want from me? I tell him to mind his own business.

THE FIRST YEAR IS coming to an end. Thanks to the series of photos of plates, I pass. The commission praises the conceptual approach, the self-reflection, the way it convinces as a series; during the assessment they call students with a less favorably judged project forward to publicly compare our work. This too is embarrassing, albeit in a different way. I'm embarrassed by my success, playing it down in front of my fellow students. This time you don't put in an appearance.

After the assessment, we end up in the Duke. There's a lot of drinking and when my supervisor, the graphic designer with the goatee, puts his arm around my waist I squeeze my glass hard. His beer gut is pressing against my side, his breath rises from a brackish well. I've passed, almost everyone has passed, I'm not complaining, everyone is drunk, look at us, we've made it over the first hurdle.

When I tell you about it later on the phone, you answer curtly that I have to learn that success comes at a price. You're going to a house on the Portuguese coast for the summer with people I don't know, we'll see each other again in September. In second-year photography, which you teach.

I'm too surprised to react. Without any warning, the summer stretches out before me, long and pointless, a swimming pool without any water.

"Have a good time, M.," you say. "Make sure you relax a little."

AFTER A FEW RUDDERLESS, uncomfortable days with my family, the boy and I bump into each other on a night out in S., the town we used to hang out in every weekend until a year ago. I go there with a friend from high school and within a quarter of an hour we both regret it, we have so little to say to each other. She disappears onto the dance floor and then completely.

Ugo is his name. Without an *H*, because of an Italian grandfather. Surprised, we clink our Bacardi and Cokes, which we've both ordered out of habit. He's taller than I remember, maybe I only used to see him from a distance. I'm taller than he remembers, he says he didn't know I had eyes like this. I tell him I bought them last year, does he want the address? We laugh. He has large hands with strong fingers, knows everything about birds, and is studying English in another town that's just as small. We're both the oldest, even if he's a little younger than me. He too has left his neighborhood, come back for the summer, and noticed that the family home has shrunk, that his brother and sisters are stuck in the past, still talking about the same things, and that his mother thinks she's cooking his favorite meal. We mock our old life mercilessly but we don't mean it badly. He touches me near my ear. I touch his forearm. We kiss in the tacky corridor next to the cloakroom and turn into impatient animals on the spot.

He comes to my room in D. with me, I go to his room in N. with him. We compare the vile kitchens and the steamed-over bathrooms, we ride our bikes through the empty town centers. I want to constantly bite him everywhere and that's allowed, he wants to constantly take everything off and that's also allowed, we don't hold back at all, we don't need any cover. It doesn't matter what time of day, the houses are empty and the beds, tables, showers, and sofas will do. He talks constantly while we're doing it; I tell him to shut up for once and we both get the giggles; afterward it's even better. Sometimes, when we're finished, he cries. I take photos of him from directly above, he's lying on the stained sheet avidly and symmetrically and I photograph him like my series of plates without realizing it. I photograph him normally and his eyes are like water. I describe a Robert Mapplethorpe portrait of Patti Smith to him, how she said that looking at it, she didn't see herself, but them.

We're outside the world, outside time. I tell him about Lee Miller in Hitler's bathtub and he says, "The things you know." We make cocktails and eat chips straight out of the packet. We write sayings and declarations and promises on each other's backs with our fingers and read them with our skin. We sit in a park and wait breathlessly for a robin that comes within a couple of feet of us. We see signs everywhere. He reads "I Have a Dream" to me and it moves him. Later he wants to do something with it, maybe he'll do law after English.

Besides the deserted D. and N., we don't go anywhere. We don't hitchhike to Berlin, we don't Interrail to Greece, we don't even pop down to Belgium for a rock festival, we just go to his terrace house in N. to watch the bickering gulls, or to the Alhambra supermarket in D., where the owner greets me with surprise. Am I the same girl who only ever used to come in for oranges and lemons?

. . .

AFTER EIGHT WEEKS, HIS classes start and I go back to my room. Eight weeks. Then the telephone rings once again for the first time, stops, and rings again. On my new schedule I see that I have a class with F. da Silva every Tuesday. After nine weeks, I drop in at your place again on a Friday night. There are some new people there, others have disappeared. You raise your eyebrows when you see me. "You look so . . . different." You take a Polaroid of me. "Have you put on weight?"

I make up a different summer. I wonder what possessed me and convince myself that this can't go on, that these two worlds can't mesh, that this simple happiness is too easy. Too bourgeois. Two days later I write to Ugo.

He phones, writes back, long letters, short letters, cards with a single question: Why? Why, why, why? He comes to D., stands on the sidewalk in front of the house and on the other side of the street, I don't open the door, I barricade myself inside, I make sure I'm not there, I tell Daniel that he mustn't let him in. I bite into towels and my knuckles, there is no why, there's nothing to understand. It was an impulse for a different life, the happiness was too ordinary. I don't say a word to anyone and leave Ugo behind in the summer.

———

THERE'S NO DENYING YOU'RE a good teacher.

The classroom is dark and there's only one slide in the carousel: *Boulevard du Temple*, captured by Louis Daguerre in 1838. We're seeing the picture for the first time, our heads are empty shoeboxes. We shuffle in through semidarkness, the room lit only by the light from the gritty boulevard, the scratched sky. You're sitting next to the humming projector, not speaking. "Narrative Techniques" is the module, this is the first class. You wait until we've sat down at the long tables, then remain silent for the first fifteen minutes before asking us, from the back of the room, who is familiar with this photograph and its history. Kamiel raises his hand and is asked to leave the room, which he does, surprised. You ask us to describe the image and we do, bit by bit. The curve in the road, the light that is probably morning light, a building whose roof is under construction or is being demolished, another roof with a strange cage on it. Paris, probably? You don't answer. The young trees that are out of focus, maybe catching the wind, the pattern in the cobblestones, which must be very bumpy, otherwise they wouldn't be so clearly defined. The viewpoint of the photographer: probably on a roof or looking through a high window. We describe every detail, every scratch, we look.

Of course you already know that we're going to overlook the most important thing, which you finally point out on the screen with your long hand so that we can no longer not see it: the two human figures at the lower right. Shapes that nobody noticed, something that looks like a pump, a blur next to it, yes, maybe a man, it could be, now you mention it.

"The first human captured in a photograph," you say. Two people, to be exact, a bootblack and his customer. The shoeshiner is sitting on a box next to a sapling; we don't recognize the merged forms as a person. The customer has his foot on the box, his hands behind his back. It wouldn't even be implausible to think that the slight tilt of his head indicates a conversation, an exchange. You tell us how Daguerre must have stood at the window of his studio with his invention—a silver-coated copper plate treated with iodine to make it photosensitive—and how it had to be exposed to the light for several minutes. How the image etched itself into the plate and was then made visible with mercury fumes—we can forget the process as long as we remember the inventiveness, the searching, the trial and error, and the triumph when it succeeded. You tell us that a historian of photography called his invention "a mirror with a memory"; the term sticks in my mind because it's so wonderfully spooky. Only the things that didn't move during the long exposure time were preserved on the plate: the street, the buildings, the trees, the bootblack and his customer. It's a nondescript blur of immense significance: For the first time in the history of the world, a real, real human has been recorded in a real, real moment.

Then you get us to imagine all the things that might have happened during those minutes on that boulevard, a large street "in a city bigger than we know here at this moment. Use your imagination," you say. We're in that city and it is definitely busy that morning. There must be carriages, carts, workers, people hurrying to their places of employment, going into stores, delivering chickens or bottles or sacks of coal, maids on errands, men in top hats and women in wide skirts. You have us fill in the street; we furnish it with stories and passersby, a carriage skirting a hole in the road, a flight of pigeons in the sky. A man holds up a hand to hail a cab, gets in, and leaves, all in those few minutes when the shutter is open. A shiver runs down my spine. I hear the wheels on the cobbles, the flutter of wings, and a wind from 1838 blows through the room—I don't know if others feel it too, I'm too shy to mention it.

"Everything is contained here in this image," you say. "It's all here," and we're not sure what you mean by that. Everything is there in that photo, and everything is here? OK, maybe. You don't tell us what we have to learn or why this is supposed to be a "narrative technique." But after this class I walk through town and feel the forms of what has just passed by, the ghosts of people and dogs who have also crossed these streets, and things that have fallen out of pockets and been picked up by someone else. I even imagine I can feel the things that still have to happen. For days, an expanded consciousness hovers over me like an outsize, weightless overcoat.

THERE IS NO HISTORICAL order or logic to your lessons. You start with Daguerre, maybe that's starting at the beginning, but the very next week you bring in magazines: *Time, Life, Paris Match, Vrij Nederland*. You teach us the difference between looking and seeing. One day you consider the pitiless photos of psychiatric patients at the Hôpital de la Salpêtrière, as terrified as caged animals, yet forced to look into the camera, and you hold forth about voyeurism and narratives without a main character.

Afterward, as a balm, you give us Ata Kandó's *Dream in the Forest*, in which Kandó's own children wander through the black-and-white Alps as elves. After the light has gone back on, someone asks if it's ethically responsible, doing something like that with children. Shaking your head, you snap at him, he's clearly missed the essence. Understood nothing of the moment when an action becomes sublimated, or the moment a person becomes a character. The moment when reality stops being reality, that's what you're talking about.

You take a step back. We're going too fast, you say. You want us to learn the distinction between looking and seeing, so that we come to understand that you can only capture something you can really see. It sounds like an enormous responsibility, a skill not everyone can master. In concentrated silence, we do your exercises and notice that we're getting better at it.

We dedicate two classes to the French artist Sophie Calle, who encounters a man called Henri B. at an opening, a man she doesn't find particularly attractive or interesting. But when he tells her that he is traveling to Venice, she knows immediately that she is going to follow him. She takes the night train to Venice, calls hotel after hotel to find out where Henri B. is staying, and, once she's tracked him down, defies the inclement weather by standing watch in the street until he appears and she can begin the pursuit she will maintain for several days. Her photos are like a private eye's grainy long-distance shots, a man seen from behind, almost disappearing into a crowd or around a corner, into arcades or over bridges. She goes where he goes, she photographs him and she photographs what he photographs, and she keeps notes of it all. It is alienating to see how vacant her pictures are and how tense it all is. With this work too, you refuse to entertain critical questions. It's not up to us to form a moral judgment about how far a photographer is allowed to go. If you really want to say something, you have to be shameless, you say. Anyone who has misgivings about that is in the wrong place.

During your classes, you never give me any sign of recognition. Sometimes you call the same evening and get me talking again and you never mention that day's class. We're different people then, in different capacities.

—

IN THE FALL YOU take me to Amsterdam with you. You want to go to the Stedelijk Museum and "into town." At the museum, it turns out that you've reserved something from the library and have an appointment with a curator. You send me off into the building like a child, with instructions to be back in ninety minutes. Unaccompanied, I drown in the collection, where I still recognize too little. The retro-modern restaurant is full of old people eating cake. In the video room under the stairs, I watch black-and-white videos by Bruce Nauman, including one of him bouncing his testicles on his hand. Keeping a straight face while viewing sexual organs in the company of other museum visitors is new to me. After that I hang around in the sunnily lit Sandberg wing for a while, where the reassuringly abstract work of American minimalists is on display. The clear corners and bright colors fill me with a fresh, clean sense of space I am keen to discuss.

But when I see you again, you don't feel like talking, something's ruined your mood. You lead the way to the inner city with long, irritated strides, while I trot along at your heel like an unwanted dog, wondering what I can do or say to improve the atmosphere. You come round by yourself; like always, beyond my influence. We walk a short distance through a wet Vondelpark, across Leidseplein, which I always imagined as an open square with rounded corners, not this busy intersection crisscrossed by tram lines, then go to Laura Dols and Zipper, well-known secondhand clothing stores. You call it "vintage" and don't need anything yourself, we're here for me, you say. I still haven't shed the idea that used clothes are shabby and dirty, though I do realize that's a narrowminded thought I mustn't say out loud. Your entourage only ever wears clothes you can't buy new.

Zipper is musty, but the two girls who work there ignore the smell. They've descended from an intimidating planet. One, thin with blond spikes and wearing a tuxedo, is leafing through magazines next to the cash register while smoking through a cigarette holder.

The plump girl who dresses me has a beehive, eyeliner halfway to her temples, and bulging pink-glazed lips that look like a separate object stuck to her face. She has dressed her ample body in a dirndl, but still doesn't come across as a Tyrolean parody. In their fingerless lace gloves, her hands gently push and pull on my now thin body, arranging me in front of a mirror. "Good bones," she says, while helping me into a man's suit, a corset, several turtlenecks, a lace blouse, a black high-necked Chinese dress with embroidered dragons on it, a completely threadbare pair of jeans she's brought up from the cellar she keeps descending into on a tiny spiral staircase—you reject the jeans—and keeps saying that everything suits me. You buy it for me, along with a leather coat I actually find too heavy. "It makes a real artist of you, M.," you say. In the mirror I see, in order, a Marlene Dietrich incarnation, a sexy woman, an existential wannabe, a Victorian virgin . . . A masquerade that has nothing to do with me personally, the identities hang off me as if I'm a cardboard dress-up doll. It's creepy and divine. You take Polaroids and that doesn't strike me as anything out of the ordinary. Everybody's taking them all the time now, "while you can still get the film."

I don't ask what I owe it all to, that would be ungrateful, and you seem to be enjoying the session whatever the reason. You're studying me with the expression you had while doing my portrait, as if you're looking at me as a form, not a character. You say it's time to develop style and I believe you. At home I hang the clothes in a separate row in my small wardrobe, a group of strangers who have come to visit.

Before I dare to wear them, I take photos, stacking the folded garments and photographing the pile from above surrounded by my old clothes, just as I did with the plates on the kitchen table. I remove one item at a time from the top of the pile to make the second series that can count on some degree of approval at school.

In one of your classes you discuss the work of Francesca Woodman, a photographer who is gaining a posthumous reputation. In her self-portraits—blurred splotches in rooms with peeling wallpaper—she wears the kinds of tops and dresses I saw on the racks of those stores. Or else she's naked, though that sounds much too concrete for such a ghostly presence. I get so cold, so cold at seeing her fleeting image, hanging off a doorjamb or crawling on the floor with nothing but her thick head of hair to protect her. In 1981, at just twenty-two, she stepped out of the window of her studio. You mention that as a sidelong comment, a footnote.

In the weeks afterward a few classmates go to a derelict house and an abandoned factory on the outskirts of town to take photos of each other. It's fall, cold, they have goose bumps and small, hard nipples in every shot. When they show me the photos I'm relieved, but tell them I wish I'd gone with them.

I DON'T SEE WHAT'S happening, I don't feel it, I don't understand it. Maybe I don't want to feel it and I don't want to know about it—how could I? Your attention and the place in your universe that has been thrown into my lap are flattering, they feel like progress. I don't dare to think in terms of love or friendship, or dependence and advantage, those words are too big and I'm still too young, but sometimes I picture the potted plants on the windowsill of my elementary school, transplanted one summer by the teacher into bigger pots with more earth, and how they grew in all directions, searching and groping into the space they suddenly perceived.

It's also comfortable, as I begin to notice. Your attention provides protection from the surreptitious hunting season that has now opened on my fellow students. With the theory instructor resting his meaty hand on the back of your neck after drinks. The life drawing instructor from the foundation year presenting himself as everyone's best friend the moment they've moved up a year and are no longer his direct student, turning up at their house parties uninvited. The philosophy professor, late forties and sweaty, arranging one-on-one sessions where he displays a deep interest in the metaphysical background of our work and especially the way it expresses our urges—analyses that often end up with his own, dry marriage. It's all there, but it remains at a manageable distance, I'm surrounded by an invisible shield.

"You're one of Flo's," says Marieke, a pretty girl from South Limburg who is pursued by all of them, sometimes simultaneously. "They don't do that with you."

⌒

ALL OF A SUDDEN a new book has been announced. Nobody except Robbie knew you were working on something. That's how you did it the other times too, you say.

"I never talk about a work until it's done, M. You have to learn to do that too; talking about it interrupts the creative process."

The invitation arrives in my letter box two weeks before the presentation. It's called *The Making of* and the card doesn't go into any more detail. With the title printed in a classic serif font on creamy white handmade paper, it's more like the cover of a novel than the announcement of an exhibition or a book of photography. It could also be the announcement of a wedding. Inside the folded card is a loose black-and-white photo of clothes on a floor: a pair of jeans, a simple striped T-shirt, cheap sneakers. Clothes I could have once worn . . . Does that really not flash through my mind?

The book presentation is going to be held in early spring in the big bookstore on the square, where there will also be a small exhibition. After that there will be a tour of other bookstores, the photography museum in Rotterdam, and an Amsterdam gallery. I see the invitation as a step up, apparently I'm becoming part of a different circle, a more inner circle, moving on from the armchair in the corner of the room.

On an impulse I phone my parents. I've been excluding them now for one and a half years; introducing them to the work of one of my teachers might be a good, serious way of involving them in my new life or preparing them for my future—or whatever possesses me. We arrange to go to the presentation together. "We'll have already eaten," my mother says. "Your sisters are busy with school."

Walking to the bus station in the twilight, I feel the bangs Robbie gave me the day before brushing against my forehead. It was your idea and I don't question your ideas. Freshly cut like this, with all the hair exactly the same length, it feels like a wig. Will they recognize me? I wonder. When I arrive, I see a couple standing to one side in thin raincoats, arms locked and looking lost. It takes a fraction of a second, but still too long, before I see that it's them.

I'D LIKE TO DELAY now, Flo, delay on the sidewalk. Turn on my heels while telling this, not go in. Just walk away from the glass door with the wooden Art Deco festoon across the panel, not ring the jingling doorbell.

THEN I WOULDN'T HAVE to step over the high doorstep into the full light of the bookstore. I wouldn't see the group of people turn toward me and smile widely, synchronized like a single organism. I wouldn't need to hear the whispering go rustling through the group like the pages of a telephone book shooting away under a thumb. I wouldn't have to see the table to the left of the entrance with the stacks of books. I wouldn't see that the book has the same format as your other titles, rectangular and not too large, stylish. That's what books of photographs look like now, with soft covers and page-filling photos alternating with very small ones, like passport photos. The title is printed on the front in wide, flat capitals, the title that doesn't even register yet.

I wouldn't have accepted the glass being offered to me by the bookstore's blushing intern, red wine in a Duralex glass, I wouldn't have spotted you at the back of the bookstore in your long, green, velvet dress with the low-cut back, I wouldn't have seen Robbie and the two feline sisters who never talk to me but now say, "Hi, sweetie," and, "Nice suit," before turning away from me. I wouldn't have rolled easily through the crowd to the back, where the small exhibition has been set up and where the title would now reveal itself to me in its full glory, along with the realization that there's only one person in all of those photos, a person who is no more and no less than a solitary letter. I wouldn't read the title and everything wouldn't become clear to me in a single thunderclap. I wouldn't want to dissolve on the spot, I wouldn't feel my stomach sinking out of my body and sliding away, slithering over the bookstore's checkered wooden floor, lost between the dropped peanuts and the beautiful shoes, a lost stomach that makes way for a body-filling heart that beats with sharp, hard blows. I wouldn't need to realize that the title, with its "..." now filled in, can only mean one thing,

The Making of M.,

that it's me, all me and everywhere, only me, me, me, me,

I wouldn't need to turn to my parents, who have been pulled out from between the protective cover of one of their three photo albums and deposited here in this company and are now looking around, their glasses of wine untouched in their hands, asking themselves if they're seeing what they're seeing, part of the whispering too, there's the parents, yes, you can see that.

I wouldn't need to see that this has all been a plan from the beginning, a project; look for a malleable young subject, not too striking and not too talented and not too smart but not stupid either, somebody . . . not a coddled rich kid but not poor either, someone with a modicum of talent but not too much and above all: living up till now in the shadows, yes, precisely that. Someone you can teach something to, someone who is green enough, who you can put in a nursery pot and water, then calmly wait to see how they grow, a bit of pruning here and there, a bit of fertilizer and pinch off a few unwanted buds, then see how they photograph, what they're worth.

THERE ARE POLAROIDS, ORDINARY photos, the portraits—a lot more than I've seen being made, very different ones too. I've been followed and recorded everywhere. There I am sitting in the corner of the room, quiet and vague among the beautiful people, who only appear on the edges as hips, hair, shoulders. There I am getting out of your car. There I am standing at the end of the line waiting for the assessments to start, feeling sick to my stomach by the looks of it, my face white and frightened. I'm isolated, you make sure there are never any other faces in the picture, and if there are, they're motion-blurred or vague like a curtain in the foreground. There: a series seen from behind, walking down the street in front of you, Flo, in moments I don't remember. You followed me or had me shadowed, is that it? The silhouette grows thinner: from bashful schoolgirl to something that kind of resembles a model, from a silhouette from the new suburbs with ill-fitting tapered jeans and Duran Duran hair to something that can pass for cute in the gloom of a club but not really in the daylight.

From Marie to M.

I see echoes, very, very vague echoes of Edie Sedgwick, of Nico, people I know from your books, but then Dutch and never rising above provincial Holland.

There is video too. A small monitor is playing footage from a security camera, obviously aimed at my front door. I see myself, synchronized on four split screens, emerging from my front door over and over again, each time slightly differently, over one and a half years. Robbie across the road, now I understand. He must have installed the camera and focused it on my front door. All he had to do was change the tapes now and then, it was so easy. There are also photos from that position; I come through the door shyly, as if it hurts to step into the light.

I stare at myself from all sides, with more and more black smeared around my eyes. It's pathetic, it's pitiful, a caricature of someone becoming an adult. Someone who's trying really hard to fake it. Are these the loneliest images I've ever seen?

I see my parents looking at the photos and at me, they don't dare to ask any questions. It must be art, they can't judge that, they thought I wanted to become a photojournalist, something useful, with a newspaper, perhaps, or otherwise in advertising. . . . I down a glass of wine and then another, and another, and all this time your green dress keeps disappearing behind other people. I haven't been able to say or ask anything and what could I?

But the worst, the worst, the very worst is the telephone on the wall that is part of the presentation, which somebody now hangs up so I can have a go, gesturing invitingly. I put the receiver to my ear and hear my own voice. Incoherent snippets of vacant chatter, a chain of everyday details, what I did, who I saw, what I ate, what I've been reading, all the things you drew out of me. Everything has been taped and edited into a mush of daily concerns. Going on about the state of the kitchen, tension about work I'm having trouble completing, demonstrations I'm not going to go to, or will, or maybe not after all. Moaning about instructors' remarks, babbling about books I clearly haven't read. Complaints you listened to, but we don't hear you on the tapes. I don't even need to look at the book to know that I will find the horrific transcription of this gushing inanity there in its own little section, with beautiful typography, and that in black and white on the page it will be even worse, even more stuttering, even falser.

I don't even have to hold the book in my hands to know what will be written about it later: how you've caught the times by the tail, what it is to become an adult in this era, this search for direction, this forming of a formless creature. That the border between fact and fiction has been suspended, that *The Making of M.* stands for the path we all have to follow, this pupation of a caterpillar on its way to becoming a butterfly, so much more boring and ordinary than it is in the animal kingdom. That the care you put into your task is beyond belief, a step further in an oeuvre characterized by its anthropological eye, this study of us, your own kind, through one young person, straight to the heart, four stars.

"SURPRISED?" YOUR GREEN DRESS, the reflection on your jawline, your clay face, and your narrow eyes. The emptiness behind them.

. . .

MY PARENTS FIND IT interesting and unusual and "special," and they don't stay long. Nobody spoke to them, nobody wanted to ask them anything—yes, the bookseller, if they'd like to buy a book. They decline politely and disappear, tring-tring goes the doorbell as they leave the bookstore, this temple of civilization. They disappear into the now dark city, to the station and then back to their apartment on a late bus.

⁓

IN SOME CULTURES TAKING a photo is seen as stealing the soul. It's an oft-repeated claim, but the origin is unclear. One time it's Native Americans, another "African tribes," then you'll hear someone say it of the population of the Andes or the inhabitants of Tahiti. It's like the hundred words for snow in the language of the Inuit or the existence of the Bermuda Triangle; dubious assertions you can never completely discount.

"The photograph," you quoted from a slim book by the philosopher Roland Barthes while walking to and fro in front of the class, "is dangerous." He even called photos gluttonous. They turn the photographed person into an object.

What is an object? A thing, something without a soul.

That's how simple it was. You had already announced it, but I didn't understand until it happened.

⁓

WE BOTH KNOW HOW this plays out, Flo. We don't speak that evening. I don't have any words, I've lost my tongue. Yes, I have a tongue to swallow wine with, glass after glass after glass. And the more I drink, the clearer everything becomes. I see that making the book has rounded off your project. It's finished. I'm finished. This will be the end of the invitations, the books, the excursions, the telephone calls. It's got a cover on it, it's been completed. There are even prospective successors, they're standing there in the corner, twins from the foundation year. Two young guys who could be choirboys, four blushing cheeks, completely identical, ideal material. You've invited them and now they're making their debut, whereas I, with the publication of your third major project, have become old news. What a magnificent book they'll make, what an incredibly fascinating series of photos, undoubtedly. They don't know it yet, their eighteen-year-old blue eyes are shining, what a fascinating group of people, what a world. I drink and drink and Erick with *ck*, the guy who writes columns, is the only one who talks to me, even if I have no idea how the words rolling out of his mouth are supposed to fit together. He's going to write about it, I understand that, right? I drink more and throw up in the bookstore toilet, flushing it away neatly. See? I don't even have a talent for debauchery, *Frau ohne Eigenschaften*; I go back and take another glass, and another, and finally succeed in finding the exit. Robbie, who's standing at the door, presses a book in a clear plastic bag into my hands.

"She's signed it," he says.

I find my way back to my shared house, where I stand in front of the door for a long time, swaying, searching—keys, where are you—pushing my hands deep into the pockets of the suit you bought me. It takes too long, too long to keep it all in. I vomit again, now in the bookstore bag. In its white linen, the flexible book bathes in a ruby-red, splashing puddle, the *M.* in the title gets a dunking. Then I throw the book in the garbage container, and myself after it, and everything goes dark.

TWO DAYS LATER I come to. Daniel picked me up off the doorstep and got me into bed; it's good I don't weigh very much, he says. He makes chicken broth from stock cubes and doesn't pry. I take the kitchen shears, bunch my hair together, and hack it off. The parody of Rod Stewart I see in the mirror will have to do.

I throw out the clothes.

I call school and tell them I won't be coming back, family circumstances.

I cancel my student grant and sign up with Randstad, ready to do any job they can get me. I stick it out longest at McDonald's, home of the golden *m*, where a cap to hide under is part of the uniform. I flip hamburgers, shake their weird skinny fries into cardboard containers, scrape the red plastic trays off into big trash cans, day after day, week after week, all the time waiting for a way out.

I finally find it in the *Algemeen Dagblad* wanted ads.

Nice working family seeking reliable, quiet au pair girl.

IV

Marie, Philippe

1989–1990

13

AFTER LANGUAGE CLASS I took a small detour through the Jardin du Luxembourg. It was windy. Piles of wet brown leaves were scattered around the tall chestnut trees like dresses that had been peeled off and cast aside. The wind drove the heavy leaves forward, scouring the ground. The metal chairs that had been placed throughout the park and were always occupied looked lost. There was no sign of the people who came here for leisurely strolls, only purposeful figures hurrying along the avenues, arms wrapped around their bodies. There were a few tourists, there always were, wherever you went. They were wandering between the trees and around the pond, maps fluttering in their hands. The children's sailboats had been lifted out of the water and stored away.

On Boulevard Saint-Michel I went into one of the many bargain clothes stores in search of something warmer to wear. While trying on a baseball jacket and a pair of jeans (you would have been sure to disapprove of them, Flo), I was overcome by a pleasant feeling and it wasn't just the material closing around my body. On the other side of the thin curtain a customer and a salesgirl were talking—an exchange about the weather and how cold it was and if they had any pants with narrower legs and the question socks in loafers, yes or no—and I realized that, without thinking and without translating, I had understood everything.

. . .

FOR ALMOST THREE MONTHS I'd been soaking up the language, absorbing it, breathing it in. Michel Dufour, the teacher who now wore a sweater vest over his drab shirt, had no time to check how well stocked our verbal pantries were. He just kept expanding and adding. I learned the vocab by heart but didn't recognize the words when I encountered them in the wild; I drilled myself in the grammatical rules but didn't yet apply them; I repeated the formulations of the children, the baker, Laurence, and the movie posters in the Metro (*Retour vers le Futur II* was about to be released) and thought I would be knocking on this door forever. I was making slow progress with reading, but the spoken language had remained impenetrable.

And now, suddenly, unannounced on a cold morning, I had ears that worked. I emerged from the fitting room in my new jacket and with my legs covered, asked if I could keep it on, paid, made a remark about the weather, and said goodbye as I strolled out of the store—without needing to think about any of it.

At last, an opening had appeared in the wall of language. On the boulevard, two women walked past complaining about their boss, an interfering new colleague, the sudden cold. I turned and followed them for a while, soaking up their grievances. I dawdled behind a man at the newsstand; in between placing his order, he asked after the newsdealer's dog, discussed the weather, grumbled about the socialists, bought cigarettes for a friend. The newspaper headlines slipped straight into my brain. The newsstand's transistor radio crackled out the news: Germany, it was about Germany again. The signs all said the same as before, the enormous ads on the curved walls of the Metro, the announcements, the bustle and din—but now without a filter. I heard everything, I read everything, understood everything.

THIS SENSE OF ENLIGHTENMENT stayed with me for days, weeks even. The Metro rides were completely different because I was constantly hearing and understanding conversations, able to apply new words to things and invent new lives for my fellow passengers in this new language. There, that woman with the exhausted expression, she was on her way home from a night shift cleaning an office and would get there just in time to take her child to school. That long-legged girl near the pole, who got off at George V station— she must have been a model on her way to her first shoot. Opposite me, in a cramped car with brown leatherette bench seats that faced each other: a woman with an ingeniously twisted tower of African wax print fabric on her head, a queen with deep purple lipstick on her downturned lips. She was undoubtedly thinking that it stank in here and she was right. The guy next to her kept touching the top of his head, midtwenties and already scared of losing his hair. A fortysomething in a suit that was creeping up his legs: I imagined him in charge of computerizing a company, cajoling its reluctant employees.

If I couldn't find a subject, I tried it out on myself. That girl, the young woman over there, the inconspicuous one with the pinched face and bony knuckles, a German or Swedish au pair, no doubt, possibly a student . . . The language poured in. Sometimes I woke up with the realization that I'd been dreaming in French.

IT WAS JUST IN time. Just in time to understand what was happening in the world. On November 9, at the end of the day, a press conference with Günter Schabowski, spokesman of the East German Communist Party, appeared on the small TV in the Lamberts' living room. He was a gray man in a gray setting saying something unbelievable, dubbed by an excited French presenter: Citizens could now, *sofort*, *immédiatement*, travel between East and West. The Wall was opening.

While the TV screen showed the journalists running out of the pressroom to spread the word, Nicolas slid across the floor on his knees to play with his cars and Philippe came into the living room.

Together we watched the few available images, which, supplied with French commentary, kept being repeated. The fall of the Wall, the end of the Iron Curtain, it was *incroyable*. Even Philippe seemed moved, sitting down, standing up again, pushing his hair back out of his eyes, and saying it was incredible, yes, incredible. He hadn't seen it coming, November 9, November 9, he hadn't anticipated it, that was poor of him. . . . A weird way to respond to world news, I thought.

After work, I didn't go to my room, why would I? I might have been in the wrong city for this great event, but it was still a metropolis, something I now realized fully for the first time. I took the Metro to Place de la Bastille, going to one revolutionary square to experience another—as a newcomer it was the best I could come up with, I'd never been there before. On the square the traffic was circling in the sodium light of the streetlamps. As if the world we knew hadn't disappeared forever into the trash can of history. I looked for a bar with a TV and found one in Rue de Charonne.

It was full enough to go in alone, and there, seven hundred miles away from the Wall, I watched the Germans climbing over it, hacking holes in it with small hammers, and prizing out bits with their nails. Some of them laughing euphorically, others dragging their feet as they crossed the border through gates they'd opened themselves. The border guards stood idly by, absolved of their task. "So, I can go visit my parents?" a woman with teased hair asked one of them. And when he said "Ja"—*Oui*, the emotional commentator translated—she kissed him full on the mouth (in the bar a cheer went up, "Oui! Oui!" every time they repeated the footage). People with ashen, happy faces cried on TV, applauding for no one in particular and everything at once. Each passing car was met as a liberator, while the civilians inside were just as astonished. A woman in a red Lada said it was beyond her, *Mir ist schlecht, J'ai mal au coeur*, I feel sick.

The French evening news featured a baffled East Germany specialist. He looked like he'd been hauled out of bed, his sui: was that crumpled. I understood every word, or thought I did, which amounted to the same thing, and meanwhile I counted my francs and ordered a 1664. I turned to raise my glass to the person next to me at the bar, a small, attractively wiry man who looked like he'd walked down from the mountains, young but leathery. He smelled of sage and was missing one of his eyeteeth.

"You must be a German," he said.

"Close," I replied.

It wasn't difficult to clink glasses, to share the happiness. It wasn't difficult to let him give me a light either, and buy me another beer. And then pretend that I no longer had any direct family, all killed in a car crash, very sad, yes, and that I was now living with a distant aunt from a branch of the family that had moved to France. I suspect he'd figured out that not a word of it was true, but neither of us cared. Stories are valuable too. He was called Luc and I was Lucy, what a coincidence.

"Imagine what it's like to suddenly step into another existence," he said, nodding sideways at the television. "Having a different world within walking distance, one you've heard all about but never been able to visit. And then they just remove the door."

"That's a fairy tale," I said. Thinking for a moment, a very brief moment, of your front door and touching my short hair. We toasted again, to that and falling walls. That night I slept for the first time in a bed in Paris that wasn't provided by my employers, a gamble that turned out well, messy and lighthearted, not necessarily an occasion to exchange addresses.

When I heard the street sweepers spraying the unknown street in the morning, the noise closer than in my own room, I slid the bottles and ashtray aside, zipped up my jeans and jacket, and walked out into the morning. It really was as easy as crossing a defunct border. At home I found a telephone number in my pocket after all, *Luc pour Lucy*, and pinned it to the door.

14

OUR STORY WAS PACKED away in a graph-paper notebook in a box with a lid on it at the bottom of a wobbly wardrobe on the eighth floor. Was it our story, Flo? It was a story, undeniably, but who it belonged to now that it had left me was not as clear. I put away the pens; it was time for me to go out into the world.

I REMEMBERED THE PHOTOGRAPHER at Laurence's sister's wedding and the ease with which he'd used his camera. When I'd arrived in Paris three months earlier, I'd slid my Pentax under the bed. Getting it back out now, it seemed like a stranger, an ex at best. But the camera still fit my hand perfectly, of course it did. My right thumb automatically reached for the lever.

A few days before, on my way to work, I'd read in a *Pariscope* I'd picked up off a Metro seat about the new monuments that had appeared in recent years, the Grands Travaux of the pint-size François Mitterrand and his minister of culture, Jack Lang, who looked like a rock star. Almost all of them had been recently completed. Just in time for the bicentennial of the French Revolution, celebrated with a three-hour burlesque parade on the Champs-Élysées with six thousand extras. The Lamberts had a videocassette of it, a gift from Grandmother Lambert, who was crazy about anything to do with the French state. I sometimes put the parade on when I was tidying the mess at the end of the day and throwing together a meal for the children. Nicolas could never get enough of it.

I had arrived a month after the celebration, which I was completely ignorant of, but the stone and glass witnesses were still there for me too. The pyramid of the Louvre had been open for half a year and the criticism (some people called it "a violation of history," eggs were thrown) had died down as the lines grew longer. The diamond pattern in the triangular glass walls spread through the city like wildfire; you saw it on posters, in advertising campaigns, on I LOVE PARIS T-shirts, and on postcards in racks at the *bar tabacs*.

I'd been there once. I'd walked between the triangular ponds at the foot of the glass pyramid, felt the water that flowed seamlessly over the bluestone edge and into a slit, and not had enough money for the admission. I did send a card of it home, cautiously reestablishing contact.

There was much more. La Géode, the *folies* in La Villette, the Grande Arche de la Défense, the Opéra Bastille, the Institut du Monde Arabe, the Promenade Plantée under construction—the Great Works were capitalized. I listed the names and addresses, marked them with crosses in the red street directory that came with the room, on maps where none of it yet existed. On my days off I didn't stay in my room and no longer tried to act like I was reading a paperback in a park. I suddenly had a different purpose. I hung the camera across my chest, put my cheap jacket on over it, and went down the seven floors. Giving yourself an assignment and carrying it out—art school may have been sinking into the past, but I'd learned something from it after all. I wouldn't photograph the people, not the residents and not the visitors. Not the couples strolling along the bank of the river, not the few children you saw in the city. Not the tramps the tourists calmly homed in on, camera at the ready, searching for the right contrast between derelict and monument. I was probably, although it was too soon to admit it, trying to avoid photographing people. Respectful or cowardly? It came down to the same thing.

I opted for motionless, new constructions. Maybe I would be able to distill the city's reinvention of itself. How change wasn't something you had to wait for. You could set it in motion yourself.

SO THAT COLD AUTUMN I wandered through the abandoned Parc de la Villette on the northeastern edge of the city, past jutting, bright red metal buildings spread at random on the bare lawns, where the young trees still had to grow, belted to thick posts against the autumn wind. It was a postmodern obstacle course, with pointless shapes and geometric paths that led nowhere. In summer the green grass, blue sky, and red accents were undoubtedly photogenic, but now the landscape was mostly graphic design.

The most intangible thing in that park was La Géode, an omniverse. A spherical picture theater clad entirely in mirrors. No matter what the direction of approach, a sphere stays a sphere stays a sphere, and this one sucked the surroundings in and spat them out again at the same time, the reflected gray sky covering exactly one half. If there were any other people walking around, the convex mirror shrank them to the size of tickling ants.

A PERFECTLY WHITE, SQUARE gate shimmered in the distance at the end of the axis that runs right through the city, the Grande Arche. A new triumphal arch. Lit at night, shining white in the daytime no matter what the weather. The thing was gigantic even from a distance. How could I have not noticed it before? One day when I had the morning off, I walked toward it from the Périphérique; the Metro line was still under construction. As I followed the road over bridges, past construction sites, and then along an endless esplanade of large paving stones toward the enormous building, it kept retreating, maintaining the same size. The town planners kept throwing barriers in my path: a half-pipe, works of art, a fountain with a light show, memorial plaques, planter boxes, another half-pipe, more works of art. Until I was suddenly standing under the arch and saw that beyond it there really was nothing else, the city came to an abrupt end. It was a gigantic square eye that looked in two directions. One side toward the navel of the old city, with the Louvre somewhere very far in the distance. In the other direction you could expect the future—but all that lay there was emptiness with a few cranes in it and an enormous cemetery. I took photos.

Was it the camera, or the time? Or the language growing more transparent? Or was it your lessons, Flo, that I was only now putting into practice? I started seeing more, including things that had been there the whole time. The vans parked on the inner ring, for instance: a long extended brothel. With the new public toilets— beige cabins with corrugated walls and rounded corners—as overflow rooms on the sidewalk.

Around the corner from my building, across the road from the parked BMWs and the uniformed embassy staff, big black women in red curly or straight blond wigs squeezed through the sliding doors of the Sanisettes with their johns. One-franc surcharge. I didn't take any photos of the women and their customers, but I did of the abandoned cabins, in the morning in the rising mist, with the thinning Bois de Boulogne in the background.

I had the rolls developed and contact prints made on the other side of the city at Objectif Bastille in Rue de Lyon, a business I had found in the Pages Jaunes. In this shiny new store, an assistant pulled the contact sheets out of the envelope and made a show of turning away discreetly, toward the glass cases with expensive cameras and rows of lenses, while I checked that they were mine.

In the small prints I studied with a magnifying glass, the city was a futuristic laboratory. Spheres, cones, cubes, pyramids; viewed through my lashes, there was nothing but geometric forms on the photographic paper, a box of building blocks upended over the old setting. Marble, glass, or plastic, lit from within or reflecting everything around them, without a past and without a conscience.

Sometimes I saw myself in those reflective surfaces, a scrawny figure with a camera in front of her face.

15

ONE DAY, JUST BEFORE Christmas, Laurence wasn't in her uniform when I arrived. She was sitting at the too-large dining table smoking with all the windows closed. Something she never did otherwise.

"Sit down," she said. I put down my bag of books; exams were coming up fast.

"The situation is . . . I have to tell you that . . ." She turned her face toward mine but didn't raise her eyes from the floor, searching for words. Her small Louise Brooks face was pinched.

Panic surged through my midriff. It had come to this. They were sending me back, it wasn't working out, they'd found someone else. I wasn't right for the boys, I didn't communicate. I had to go back to my own country. I was too old, or maybe too young, or too Dutch, even. I had to go back, but to what? This wasn't what I wanted, I had to make the best of a bad lot. This job was all I had, it was the starting block under my feet. I didn't want to go back, only forward, whatever that meant.

Laurence rubbed her nails, French manicure, company regulations.

"Philippe and I are separating."

I sat down. Laurence stubbed out her cigarette and poured herself a glass of 7 Up, raising her eyebrows at me. "Would you . . . ?"

No, that was too weird, suddenly drinking soda with the woman who only ever spoke to me in the form of instructions.

"We decided last week. It will take a while before we—" She gulped down her drink and burped behind her small hand. "Work out the living arrangements." I nodded. Everything was going to change. In the small room three steps down the hall, Louis was asleep; soon he would be stuck to my hip again like a little monkey. Soon his soft hair, smelling of lavender lotion, would be pressed against my shoulder. I could already feel the ripping as they pulled him away from me.

But she hadn't said I had to leave.

"You might have noticed that it wasn't going well," Laurence said, lighting a fresh Dunhill, tapping the table with the pack. "Philippe . . ." She hesitated. "Three years ago Philippe had a, um, an accident. *Il a eu un accident.* Since then he hasn't really been, um, the same." She was talking to the glass of the window, sending her words after the smoke. "At first we were living very differently, before the, um, accident. In a large apartment near Nation. But he couldn't keep his job."

I didn't understand what she was talking about, but nodded as she presumably expected. Now she looked at me, her round brown eyes watery.

"They found other work for him. They did that much, Renault is a respectable company. Work he could manage. And this apartment. It's quite a good neighborhood, but you know, it's small, very small."

She didn't say it to point it out to me—as if I might not have noticed—but to make it clear to me that this wasn't the intention. That this life was a mistake, a wrong turn she had never chosen. She waved her hand, taking in the entire rabbit warren in a single gesture.

"Things were very different at first, he wasn't like this. This isn't what we wanted, what I wanted. We had a different life, a good life, you understand. It was three years ago. . . . But it can't go on like this. I have to move on, you understand. And the boys . . ."

Suddenly she looked at me as if I'd just come in.

"I'd like some coffee, Marie. And I have to make some calls, arrange things."

I stood up and put on the coffee as silently as possible. I could stay.

16

THE PROBLEMS BETWEEN MY employers accumulated. We were heading for winter, the windows stayed shut, and inside the apartment the impending divorce went round and round in circles, condensing to a substance that left even less room to move.

I wasn't unhappy, though. I think I was even slowly able to stop constantly seeing myself from a distance, above and from one side, stumbling through surroundings that were foreign to me. For the first time, I occasionally coincided with the place I was and the actions I was carrying out.

I can't describe it any other way, Flo. Once the language clicked, all kinds of other things started flowing too. Things that had seemed like a series of new and complicated hurdles—buying bread, the tempo of the language classes, the work, the commuters hurling themselves down the Metro stairs like lemmings, keeping your ticket or dropping it on the floor after using it, constantly judging which side of the street was safest for walking on in which neighborhood, depositing money in a bank account, withdrawing money from an account, fending off gangs of Roma children who suddenly appeared out of nowhere late at night in remote Metro corridors and tried to cut open your bag, the rattling jackhammers on sidewalks that were constantly under repair, bearing so much beauty and so much ugliness at the same time, the new faces wherever I went—they were now part of the stream of reality. The days were no longer individual, detached situations that demanded I remain on high alert, or describe them, or even think about them. They were starting to resemble each other. To blend together. And I was functioning.

You could call it habituation, or numbing. But it wasn't like that. While the family I worked for was capsizing, I had learned to swim. Sometimes I felt the onset of pride.

I NOW AVOIDED THE Lamberts' apartment as much as possible. As soon as Laurence had left for work, I got Louis out of bed, gave him something to drink, and dressed him. He could walk quite well by now, surprisingly fast for such a delicate child. I tied his laces, did up the toggles of his duffle coat (the French dressed their children like miniature adults), put the hood over his head, and brushed his lank brown hair under it with my hand. "Come on, we're going," I said. He gave me his little hand.

In the beginning I felt guilty. It was like I was kidnapping him. But a conscience is quickly assuaged: The apartment was so oppressive, it was good for his development, we had to go out anyway. Heading out soon became normal. I could say we were going for an errand, or that Louis wanted to go outside. His vocabulary was growing every day, but he still couldn't say where we'd been. Or that I'd let him skip his nap and catch it on my lap on the Metro, and that in moments like this it was like I was his mother—an extremely young one, true, but quite plausible. I planned what I would say if people spoke to me and compared our eye color ("his father is more Mediterranean"). He called me Mémé.

For a few hours, until I had to pick up Nicolas, we were free. I planned excursions with the bus timetables and relied on the regularity of the Metro lines. There were a few quiet hours in the middle of the day, and we were always back before the afternoon rush got going.

THESE EXCURSIONS ALWAYS HAD a distinct goal—today we're going to count the boats, today we're going to eat a pancake, today we're going to see the big tower—and led us through the city. We climbed the deserted steps in Montmartre, taking them one at a time, kicking aside the fallen leaves. We stood on Rue La Fayette, on the bridge over the railroad lines close to Gare du Nord, pointing down at the trains. With Louis on my shoulders, I strolled over Père Lachaise cemetery, we waved at the mournful statues and listened to a German guitarist playing at Jim Morrison's grave in the middle of a knot of quietly weeping fans. "Riders on 'ze' Storm." It was crawling with cats and we hissed at them.

We often took the bus along the Petite Ceinture and I left it to Louis to decide where we would get off, when to push the button. From the bus stop at Porte de Clignancourt, we walked along the edge of the big flea market, where the shell-game hustlers and their accomplices lightened the pockets of visitors. Then south on Boulevard Ornano, a raceway with plastic litter everywhere and a strong smell of diesel, kebab, and roast chicken. On Barbès, we studied shop windows where headless dummies were crammed together like on a railroad platform, dressed in synthetic suits and shiny party dresses, wholesale only.

Other times I moved among the tourists with my toddler. We drank tea from a thermos on the cold benches at the base of the Eiffel Tower or at the fountains on the other side of the Seine. We rode the outside escalator at the Centre Pompidou, up and down, up and down. Or I walked with him on my arm, a featherweight, through the Halles, an endless underground mall, then past the vegetable stands at the market behind Saint-Eustache. Louis waved at things and I named them; he repeated the words, mumbling close to my head.

With a child with me, I got to know the different neighborhoods in sections, step by step. Anywhere would do. For both Louis, as a new little human who'd scarcely been out of his own neighborhood, and me, the immigrant. I didn't feel inferior or superior, not out of place or too young or too old, but at home in all these situations, unobserved.

And nobody knew about it.

It sometimes happened that I had to run right up to the school exit piggybacking Louis, flushed red and arriving just in time to put him down on the sidewalk and be there when Nicolas came through the gate. He was so exhausted he never noticed anything, walking past me with a surly look or sometimes pressing his face against my stomach and bursting into tears.

"He's a handful, isn't he?" said another au pair, a girl from Ivory Coast who took three asthenic sisters home every day.

"He's not too bad. It's the home situation," I said.

I wasn't just a kidnapper, I was also airing the dirty laundry in public.

DESPITE THE COLD, I still decided to take the boys to a playground for a while. Not our usual large one, which was closed for maintenance, but "the little one" a bit farther away, a bare patch of grass among high-rise apartments, surrounded by a rusty fence. Night was falling between the buildings, which you could look under and see three streets away thanks to the Le Corbusier–style stilts they stood on—the open, friendly architecture intended to banish problems but not succeeding. Although it was only a couple of blocks away from the Lamberts', the city hadn't gone to the trouble of planting any poplars here. It was somewhere Laurence had told me to avoid, a place "foreign" children played. Once someone had jumped off a balcony here, in full view of the square. There was "trafficking."

On the square a crowd of dark-skinned boys were kicking a flat soccer ball around. The occasional sister, with dozens of little braids sticking out in all directions, had to entertain herself on the concrete slabs the loud sounds echoed off. Two large women were standing to one side and chatting in a clicking language, eyes gleaming in the blue twilight. Louis started to follow the fence with his small pattering steps, holding a stick against the bars to make a rattling sound.

It must have happened when Nicolas was slumped over the bar of the carousel and got into a fight with some other boys who wanted something—he had to get off, or they wanted to turn it faster. I left the bickering boys to their own devices for a moment. Then two of them, scarcely older than Nicolas, put on deep bass voices, suddenly sounding like the older brothers who were gathered a little farther along in the gallery. I tried to mediate, but one of the women came up to me wanting to know what I was meddling in. Big and burly in the twilight, she called me "white girl" and gave me a slow push on the shoulder. Then she turned on her heel to give one of the little boys a hard slap. I was getting into something that was over my head verbally and maybe more. Their rapid French contained words I would never learn at language school. The confrontation lasted a minute, maybe two or three. Four at most.

And suddenly I heard it. The rattling, the soft tick in the background, had stopped. HOW LONG AGO? The playground gate was open. Louis.

"Le môme," said one of the two women. "Il est pa'ti." As I turned toward them in the thick blue molasses of the twilight, no sound came out of my mouth. My whole immobile, inattentive, irresponsible body felt slow and warm, as warm as bathwater. The streetlights and the yellow lighting on the high-rise galleries flicked on, in precisely that moment, as if to emphasize what had happened: The au pair, the white girl, hadn't paid attention and now the kid was gone. Vanished, swallowed by the growing dark.

"What's his name?" The women clicked their language, the boys changed into an army on a rescue mission, shooting off into every corner of the square and playground, disappearing under the archways, spreading out on the street. Louis's name echoed off the buildings. I turned to Nicolas, breaking free from the molasses and ready with a lie, telling him that Louis was playing hide-and-seek and we had to go and look for him. Nicolas had to look with me and wasn't allowed to let go of my hand. Could he do that, OK? Like a big brother, all right?

IT'S NOT STRANGE THAT he was found. That I, imprisoned in a body that was now full of electric shocks, suddenly saw him in the distance in the space under a high-rise, framed by its spread legs. Leaning forward and scurrying, almost running, as he pushed a fluorescent pink mini-stroller, a doll's baby carriage that belonged to one of the girls. It wasn't strange either that I stuffed Nicolas's hand into a bigger boy's and covered the hundred feet that separated me from Louis in one mighty leap, lifting up his little body before he reached the sloping sidewalk that led down to the busy road and the roaring, blind-and-deaf, rush-hour traffic. It wasn't even illogical that in the blink of an eye everyone was back where they had been in the playground and carrying on where they had left off, as if the event was a piece of film that had now been cut out. The women at their post again, the boys under the arches, and Louis rattling along the fence.

No, the strange thing was Philippe showing up in precisely that moment. His coat was open, he'd been running. In the sallow light of the lamps he looked sick, with dark circles under his eyes, his hair stuck to his forehead. He stopped at the gate, telling me in a shrill voice that we had to go home. Nicolas ran up to him and grabbed his hand. Philippe scarcely noticed. He asked if everything was all right, was I sure, what were we doing here. I knew they preferred us not to come here. "Is everything all right? Are you sure? And nothing's happened? No?" He stumbled over his words and kept repeating the question. "And nothing happened? So nothing happened?"

And while I confirmed that—"No, everything's fine, we just wanted to come here for a while. Hey, Nicolas, we've been playing a fun game, haven't we?"—I saw that he was looking right through me.

Philippe knew exactly what had happened. He knew that I had let his youngest get away and that it had been a matter of seconds. He knew that I wandered the city with his child, he knew I took risks. He walked ahead of me, holding Nicolas's hand, pulling him along and looking back now and then with wandering eyes, continually wiping his face, which gleamed moistly in the light of the streetlamps. He knew all of it.

17

THE MEN FROM THE moving company carried the furniture and boxes up in an hour. The smell of their sweat and corn-paper cigarettes still lingered in the room as Laurence and I slid the heaviest things into place and plugged in the first lamps. How deceptively easy it was to relocate a life. You clicked a switch and started over.

The new apartment seemed an improvement: out of the banlieue and back into the city, a fourth-floor in Rue Victor Massé in the 9th arrondissement, south of Montmartre. A neighborhood with *commerçants*: bakers and greengrocers, a couple of guitar stores, a few brasseries with boisterous waiters, life in the streets.

But this apartment too was small. Despite its claim to be *lumineux*, most of the outside light that reached it was reflected off the blank whitewashed wall the three windows looked out on. There was no elevator, no bathtub, no indoor parking. After just a couple of days, Laurence's Renault was covered with dents from the local "kiss-kiss" parking style. In the evening the kitchen extractor system from *p'tit resto* Viva Italia on the ground floor blew the smell of oregano, cheese, and pizza crust into the rooms.

Across the corridor lived a single mom, a young Jane Birkin look-alike, who sighed "Bonjour" when we passed on the stairs but yelled at her daughter behind closed doors. An invisible trumpet player upstairs practiced for hours every afternoon.

In their new neighborhood, Laurence implored me to always, without fail, take the boys out for a walk to the south. Just a few hundred feet to the north was Boulevard de Clichy with its peep shows, live shows, drag shows, sex shops, sex video stores, girls-girls-girls, gay shows, and the Moulin Rouge in the middle. The pale red mill on the roof, large on the posters but in reality surprisingly puny, slowly stirred the exhaust fumes. The raised median strip was an extended park, the territory of tramps, dealers, fences, and emaciated men with nervous gaits.

In the daytime I was only allowed to take the route to Nicolas's nearby and well-secured school or to Square Alex Biscarre, a closed garden where sudden peacefulness hung between the tall buildings like cotton wadding. After my departure in the early evening, Laurence locked all three of the locks on the front door.

I liked it there. The higher location made the light different, the smog didn't seem as thick as in the areas closer to the Seine. There were younger people out on the streets. It was a good bit livelier than where they'd been living, but it wasn't liveliness that Laurence craved. She described it as a *solution temporaire* she'd rather not talk about. Philippe had moved back to his childhood home in Rue Marbeau; that too was temporary. Visiting arrangements were still up in the air. *On va voir*, was Laurence's comment on everything, we'll see. And also, *J'en peux plus*, I can't take any more.

MME. LAMBERT WAS STILL responsible for providing for me, the au pair—that aspect hadn't changed—so I now returned every evening from my work at Laurence's shabby apartment in the 9th to the fancy 16th arrondissement, where I climbed the stairs at the back of the big silent building Philippe had moved back into to the eighth floor, a journey that returned me to the bottom of the social ladder. I was gradually becoming adept at crossing borders, stepping through all these swinging doors, existing in all these situations simultaneously.

Now that I'd been exposed to the family so fully, there was little point in their trying to keep up appearances, and Laurence had decided that I might as well know how things stood. Either that or she didn't have anyone else to talk to. Sometimes, after arriving home, she would ask me to stay for a while and then twist the caps off two small bottles of beer. Slumped down on the new IKEA couch with its pattern of pastel lightning bolts, her thin face almost engulfed by the puffy cushions, she gradually told me more about Philippe's accident. It had actually been an attack—I must have heard at least something about it *chez moi*? In 1986? She didn't realize how much of an eternity ago that was for me.

For the first time, I heard about the bombs on the train line, the Champs-Élysées, in the post office—places I knew. Tati in Rue de Rennes; I had recently bought socks there for the fall. How quickly history erased its own tracks; they were like stories from somewhere else, from long ago.

She told me how she had seen Philippe, wounded and deathly still, in the hospital after the completely unexpected telephone call from the police. The start of a long, drawn-out process. How it was only much later that he regained consciousness, remembering nothing, at first not even recognizing her. How difficult it had been for Nicolas, how it had changed him too. There had been an au pair there as well, one of my predecessors, very young, Eloïse—a name on the wall in my room. A girl who had slept in my bed, who had looked at the same view from the same window; who had led the same little boy, only one at the time, by the hand. She had survived the attack, but seriously injured. They'd taken her back to Germany.

Laurence was talking quietly, like a robot. I couldn't work out from her words what had been worse: the injuries Philippe and the girl had suffered or his inexplicable presence in Rue de Rennes, something he'd never wanted to talk about. The hope and anxiety around his faltering recovery or the slowly growing disappointment in the year that followed, when he turned out to be damaged after all. He was constantly worried, alert, sometimes warning complete strangers on the street about nonexistent dangers. He was no longer the man she'd married; it was humiliating.

When he went back to work the effects became even more pronounced. His capacity to plan ahead was reduced, sometimes his reactions were unexpected—he'd burst into joyless laughter for no reason. He upset people. At the office he was often preoccupied, he could stare out the window for hours on end. That's how they explained it to her. Eventually Renault had put him to work in another position, or, well, how could she put it—they parked him somewhere else. Their financial position changed. Having to give up the large apartment near Nation to move to the banlieue, also arranged by Renault, where she'd been obliged to adjust her onward-and-upward expectations—that was terrible.

But she hadn't given up hope. In the end they would put it all behind them, she was still convinced of that. Louis was born, the second child she'd wanted for so long. It was good for Philippe, he seemed to stabilize and he was good with the baby, just as he'd been good with Nicolas. Maybe it would all turn out.

"UNTIL SEPTEMBER SEVENTEENTH LAST year," said Laurence. The day he'd been invited by the state to attend the inauguration of a memorial at the site of the attack, outside Tati in Rue de Rennes. They'd gone together, of course. François Mitterrand had spoken briefly and a marble plaque had been unveiled. It was a small, informal event, but the gravity of the occasion was unmistakable.

Philippe hadn't wanted to go any closer than the other side of Rue de Rennes, out of range of the press cameras. Halfway through the ceremony, which they hadn't been able to follow at all from so far away, he got confused and wanted to leave. She tried to talk him out of it, but nothing she said sank in.

"He was mumbling gibberish, looking straight through me.

He kept stumbling, it was . . . *embarrassing.*" She reached for an English word to emphasize the way she'd felt.

She looked for a taxi, but the street was closed because of the ceremony. They had to walk almost all the way to Tour Montparnasse to get one. In the taxi she'd looked at her husband, seen the way his eyes kept shooting to and fro, and realized they were back where they'd started. And she realized she'd had enough. This wasn't what she'd worked her way up from Compiègne for. It was too much for her.

"I can't do it anymore, Marie. I have to think of the boys' future, and my own. You have no idea how difficult it is here."

No, I had no idea. It seemed strangely parallel to think that this had been going on for the past few months, while I had been working with the family almost every day. Like a household appliance, now promoted to sounding board. I changed their sheets, I washed their underwear, I kept their children alive, but knew nothing about them, just as they knew nothing about me. None of us had any idea.

SO I'M STARTING OVER," Laurence said, her lips pressed together to form the line she'd drawn under the past. "Sans parking. Above a pizzeria."

18

WITH A COUPLE OF plastic bags bouncing off my calves, I descended the steep Rue des Martyrs after work in the pink late-afternoon light of spring. It was April. Not much longer and I'd be able to go out without a coat.

On the cold, dirty side of Notre-Dame de Lorette, a clochard was sitting on a pile of grayish-brown clothes with a cardboard sign in front of him saying PITIÉ. I knew him. He shuffled his textile pyramid through the neighborhood, from the church to the Monoprix exit and then outside La Rimaudière café, where they chased him off with raucous cries and where he just as stubbornly returned. Another thing about Paris: There was always somebody who was worse off, worse off than you or worse off than a random passerby, and there was sure to be someone else, not far removed, who was even worse off. It was just a question of your point of reference.

I tossed one of the coins I had fished out of a pocket or drawer at the fragmented family's into his plastic cup. His singsong refrain rose up, *Pitié, santé, soyez humain, soyez chrétien, Dieu bénisse les bienfaiteurs, merci, amen.* Something for everyone.

Around the corner, the sun was shining, a beam hitting the street with a strength you only saw here, lighting up the passersby like a spotlight in the theater. In the crowded Metro a man pressed his erection against me. I maneuvered a rustling bag between his crotch and my hip and closed my eyes until my station. The streets, the code lock, the spiral staircase.

In the corridor on my floor a stripe of light was visible on the side of my door. It was unthinkable that I hadn't closed and locked the door that morning, that was simply impossible, and yet I still naively pushed it the rest of the way open and there, in that pink spring light, was Philippe, the father, or the man who until very recently had played that role, sitting on my narrow bed. He raised both hands to stop me from screaming.

HE WASN'T GOING TO do anything. I mustn't be scared. He would be gone in a minute. He just wanted to be here for a moment. He wanted . . . No, no, don't be scared. He was on his way. Look, the door was open. He pronounced the words softly. I pressed my shoulder blades back against the cold wall.

Philippe looked terrible. I'd forgotten how quickly someone could change, how fast I myself had changed not long before, several times. The state you were in always seemed the most natural; how else could you live with yourself? (The photos in your book—that I had never looked at again and would never seek out—already had nothing to do with me. Every fiber of my epidermis had renewed itself since then and the rest would follow suit. It was that simple; what seemed fixed in those grains no longer existed. Every photo is a lie, or at best a truth that disappears the moment the click dies out—that's what Godard should have said.)

PHILIPPE WASN'T THE SAME either. So unshaven, in a crumpled shirt and with unwashed hair, he looked like a makeup artist had gone to work on him. It had been three months since his family had fallen apart and this was what it had done to him.

"It's not right for you to be here," I said.

He raised his hands even higher, as if I had a pistol trained on him. He hadn't wanted to scare me, I needn't worry, he would—

"It's not right," I said again, and cautiously lowered the bags, the plastic rustling as I put them on the floorboards. I slid toward the open door. "You should leave." I hoped that somebody would come past, but no. Farther along, my unknown fellow resident put the lambada on again, the piano accordion jangling through the hall while I calculated my chances. Philippe didn't look like he was going to do something to me, which was an absurd scenario anyway, I thought I knew him well enough for that. Although, what did I actually know? How damaged was he?

"Please, Marie," he said, "let me sit here for a moment and tell you something. I just wanted to spend a little time here." His eyes were heavy, the left eyelid drooping more than the right. "You should know, the situation . . . As an adolescent I sometimes used these rooms to study, to get some privacy when I was young. . . . Not even that long ago, if I stop to think. . . . I just wanted to sit here in this light." He gestured at the dormer window with its familiar rectangular view. In the distance, the congress center started blinking.

"The situation . . . There are things I want to tell people, things I see. . . . Will you please just sit down for a moment, let's drink a glass of water. Keep the door open and just let me talk, please. . . ."

So many years later, it's easy to be indignant or at least surprised that I didn't protest. I didn't work him out of the room. I didn't run away. You could put my behavior down to all kinds of factors: the zeitgeist, the power relationship, the paralysis that takes hold of a woman when threatened by a man, freeze or flight, concepts that didn't even exist at the time, and if they had, I wouldn't have realized that they were also applicable to me and that moment. This is what convinced me: the raised hands. The helplessness of that gesture. The time he turned up just when Louis was no longer missing, he'd come up to me in exactly the same way, with the white palms of his hands turned toward me, and he'd had the same expression. I was guilty then and he knew it, he knew that I'd almost

lost his son. He knew, and he'd never mentioned it. I owed him.
The least I could do was not start screaming.

I poured two glasses of water, put his on the floor, sat on the
kitchen chair next to the table in the corner, and listened to his
story.

"IT'S A STORY WITH a beginning and an ending. This is how it began:
The first three were born in the Hôpital Cochin. My brothers and my
sister, all three with a lower-than-average weight at birth, but otherwise real Lamberts. Self-assured. As if they have a right to everything.

"I was, as they say, 'a little different.' I paled in comparison, I
think. My mother, Ghislaine, blamed my place of birth. She thought
we should never have moved. But it suited their new status, you
see. Father had been named chairman of the board at the Ministry
of Telecommunication the year before. Director general. Boss of
the post. That's how it works in the civil service. He wore a hat, he
was a dandy. He steered clear of politics—sensible for a man in his
position. They were turbulent times, de Gaulle was gone. La Poste,
he said, had to 'plow on like a reliable steamboat'—he loved similes. It was hardly possible for a civil servant to rise any higher. A
fourth child completed the picture. Along with a larger apartment
and a different neighborhood."

It was more words in one burst than Philippe had spoken to me
in all the preceding months. I didn't understand everything, but
committed it to memory. The tension in my neck and back eased a
little. I thought of all the people in the small rooms at the same level
as us, invisible. And the pigeons above them.

"THEY MOVED HERE. A spacious five-bedroom apartment in the six-
teenth arrondissement, with a library and a salon with tall windows. This was an area with embassies, the German consulate
around the corner. At the end of the street you could see the green
of the Bois de Boulogne.

"There used to be a bullfighting arena on this site, just before the World Fair. My mother thinks that's the reason. She thought there had been too much violence on this ground, too much bloodshed. That a child feels that. It never bothered the others, my father would reply. Even though they were born more or less on top of the catacombs. It was just coincidence that I was different, he said. More sensitive, more nervous perhaps. Not something they needed to worry about. I had convulsions, they would pass. I'd land on my feet, Lamberts always did. There had never been a Lambert who didn't make a go of things."

WHILE TALKING, PHILIPPE STARED at the wall in front of him. The story had been maturing inside him for a long time. He had given the details a lot of thought, he wasn't choosing them at random. He was sketching a picture of himself, a picture that would explain to me how he had ended up here, in my room and in this state. It was a story with fixed coordinates, one that could be told and told again. Maybe he was trying it out for the first time, on me, the au pair, the reserve who would take the field briefly and then be replaced.

The situation felt like a scene from a play. I could remove a wall, take a few steps back, and watch it. I would be sitting there with the father of the family that had fallen apart, in the twenty or thirty square feet I temporarily called my own, a cocoon outside of time and space, the safest place at that moment. My discomfort about his sudden appearance had vanished. I was witness to a sack that needed to be shaken out, bit by bit, until it was completely empty, an action I understood all too well.

HE WAS TALKING ABOUT "foreknowledge" that manifested itself in his teenage years. He first noticed it in the days before his grandmother died after being hit by a bus. He had felt the imminent danger days in advance as "a kind of rustling." Not audible, but tangible.

The air vibrating around him, like water passing over your body when you're swimming. No, not like the wind, heavier and more physical than air. Like water. But then with a very light specific gravity, do you follow me? He thought of his grandmother, knew that something terrible was looming over her, something enormously large and heavy, and felt the rustling around him. But nobody wanted to listen.

His grandmother had an accident, the greyhound died a nasty death, his mother just escaped the fire in Galeries Lafayette—but still everyone kept acting like he hadn't been warning them days in advance, as if he hadn't been harassed by fearful dreams he wanted to discuss. They talked over him, changed the subject, suddenly had something else to do, and forgot his remarks.

"People see what they expect, what they want to see. Everything else seems unnatural to them and they try to prove that it is," he said. That was why they remembered the times he raised a false alarm all the better. In the eyes of his father, his brothers and sister, and even his mother, he saw doubt, a suspicion that he might not be right in the head. Oversensitive, *nerveux*. "It's knowledge that makes you lonely," he said. *Knowledge* of the future, he called it, not once did he call it *predicting* the future, or a suspicion. It was knowledge, more or less reliable, that manifested itself as a feeling on his skin. It wasn't a knowledge that could divert events or influence them.

It was no use to anyone, he said. It was a curse.

HE TOLD ME ABOUT meeting Laurence during a business flight. About their apartment close to Place de la Nation, how reassuring the hum from the traffic circle was while his life indoors took a calm direction. The birth of Nicolas and how the rustling fell silent afterward. Nothing would happen to this child, he was convinced of that—and still was, he said—but it wasn't enough to curb his fears forever, though he had long thought it would be. Laurence had never known anything about it, he hadn't wanted to worry her. She seemed so happy.

How it began again when Eloïse appeared. Her red hair, her well-nourished appearance, the green tint in her eyes, and the certainty that something would destroy all of this—a knowledge that hit him in an instant and literally brought him down.

Eloïse—the name on the wall, the fourth au pair. The girl who was quickly replaced. Who was erased.

"When I came to, I was filled with a terrible longing that it hadn't happened," said Philippe, "but I also knew that this was just the beginning." His fear had only been dormant, he said in a bitter voice, "like a patient dog waiting in front of the supermarket for its master to reappear," and now it had stood up to accompany him.

That was how he put it. I pictured the dog and resolved to remember that too.

DETAILS ANCHOR THE NARRATIVE. That's what you taught us, Flo. When you're looking through the lens, don't start by worrying about your subject. That's already there, you've focused on it, you've already captured it. No, look at what's happening around it. Look at the moving leaf that's casting shadows, at the knuckles turning white, at a crooked seam or a lost button, an open door in the background. All these things are equally important.

I memorized them while Philippe stumbled over his words, talked to his hands and the floor, switching between the English he'd learned at work and French, which no longer held any secrets for me. With all its abundance, I could follow it now through all the different future forms and the chaos of past tenses. This language seemed made for speculating and leaving chinks open to what could have or should have happened. The language also made Philippe's account more of a story than a confession.

. . .

HE TOLD ME ABOUT his work, the girl, the restlessness. About the vacation, the heat in their summer house, the sneaking around, the shame, the return to Paris. The menace, the attack, his mother's car. Shadowing Eloïse through the streets, her red hair in the distance. I committed the crumbs to memory, the cards she wrote, her cheap dress, the newspaper headlines. Again I thought how strange it was that what had happened here so recently, partly in this room, hadn't left a single trace besides her name and maybe a beer coaster under a table leg. Eloïse had left here one midday for a carefree day off and never returned.

And the city. In those weeks and months, Paris had been ruled by fear and now it was—besides the shabby rustling of the garbage bags in rings on the streets—hardly noticeable. Or did I miss the signs? I even accepted the fully armed police patrols as part of the decor. I walked through the city blindly, or should I say, blinded . . . by all the other things, the day-to-day things I had to learn to see first.

THE TWILIGHT HAD ALMOST turned to darkness. Far away, hundreds of miles to the north in my parents' apartment, my father would be closing the venetian blinds and turning on the lights. My sisters, sixteen and seventeen, would be studying for their exams, at different schools but together at the dining table. For just a second, I pictured them bent over their books, light brown hair, my youngest sister jiggling her feet while she wiggles a pen between her index and middle fingers, never able to sit still. For a second, I saw her in Eloïse's stead; it could have happened like that and it could happen like that in the future. For the very first time since leaving, I felt a pang of homesickness.

Against the wall of my room, the only patches of light remaining were Philippe's off-white shirt and the tip of his cigarette. He leaned back against the wall and repeated how everything had suddenly stopped: seeing, hearing, feeling. I switched on the table lamp, he turned away from the light. His shirt was stained dark around his armpits and on the back.

THE END OF HIS story left me dazed. I didn't dare ask any questions about it. It was too late for sympathy, and our work relationship didn't allow it either.

But there was one thing I wanted to know—why was he telling me this? He shrugged, or just shuddered.

"As an adolescent I sometimes fled to these rooms, they were empty at the time. I looked at the congress center, which was still under construction. It reassured me. It was a safe place. No rustling. I needed that."

From outside we heard footsteps on the street, heels in the night. A car door slamming, the bleep-bleep of an electronic car lock. "Renault Fuego," Philippe mumbled.

I still wanted to know. "But why me?"

"Because you're here now in this place. Because you . . ." He looked at me, his face like an old man's. "I don't know yet, Marie, I don't know for sure. There's something . . ."

There was—what?

"I think that you . . . But it's something very far away. I can't see it properly."

He stood up, drained the glass of water I had refilled, and asked if he could come back sometime. I shrugged. As if he'd asked the first time. As if my opinion made any difference.

I MENTIONED THE ENCOUNTER in guarded terms to Clara, my Spanish fellow student, who I'd been spending more time with since we'd gone for a drink together after the exams. It turned out she wasn't much older than me, her genteel appearance had created a false distance.

It was easier to wander the streets together and it was much more relaxed to be together while hanging out in the cheap bars around Canal Saint-Martin. Clara had started as an au pair too, in Montreuil, but had left the family after a couple of weeks because her employer was constantly grabbing her breasts—a variation on the story of one of the Germans and one of the Swedish girls too in the past few months. She thought I'd been lucky. "A bit cuckoo, that boss of yours, but he doesn't seem dangerous."

After working as a cleaner at a swimming pool and on the checkout at Auchan, Clara now had a job at ExactChange, a currency exchange office near the Halles, which gave her the means to rent a room in Belleville. She spent the whole day behind bullet-proof glass in a shoebox-size office explaining the current rate to tourists and confirming that they also charged commission to change their tattered paper money. "'Yes, I'm sorry but those are the rules.'

"They already know that, Marie, it's written on the front of the building in neon letters, but they still complain, they still get angry. And you have no idea how filthy some of that money is," she said, before pinching her Iberian nose and sucking on the straw she always requested with her beer. ("It works faster.") "I wouldn't be surprised if they kept it in their underpants." Dutch money, "your money," was the favorable exception and also the most beautiful money in the world, "Mother of God, it is so beautiful. Every time I see one of those sunflower notes, I stroke it."

WE SOMETIMES WENT TO a disco near République. There was a video screen and we spent the whole night hoping they'd play the clip of Les Rita Mitsouko's "C'est Comme Ça." If they did, and that was a certainty in those first, fresh months of the 1990s, we swung our heads and danced with jerky steps just like the singer's.

Clara didn't just stroke banknotes, she also stroked me when she'd sucked too much beer up through her straw. She said I smelled good, she liked the way I moved, she put her arm around my shoulders and grabbed the short hair on the back of my head when I was talking to other people, which I did without the slightest effort when I was with her. We let men pay for our drinks, then gave them the cold shoulder.

Our friendship was separate and self-contained. It was a pact, closed on the territory of the new language. I hoisted myself up on her cheerfulness and her adamantine conviction that she was going to make it here in Paris, no matter what. She thought I had taste and often I made her laugh. We didn't tell each other anything about our previous lives, we were born the day we arrived here.

Only once did she refer to a previous existence. In a crammed club close to Pigalle she grabbed my hand at five in the morning and pressed it to her sweaty chest. Her big eyes with their smudged black lines gleamed in her face, she put her mouth close to my ear and yelled over the music: "It doesn't matter, Marie, what happened to you or me, what anybody thought of us or wanted to do. We're only going forward, *on y va, direction tout droit.*" On her platform heels and without backward glances, she was going to stroll straight into the future. It belonged to her and now it was mine too, even if we, like most people in their early twenties, couldn't see anything concrete there yet.

All this had grown over the past few weeks, naturally, without my having to decide anything or be surprised by it.

"And this guy only talks to you?" she asked. "You're lucky, Marie, really. Next time ask him to pay you for it."

I ONLY SAW PHILIPPE in passing. He stayed in his childhood home on the fourth floor, *solution temporaire.* His mother was spending all of her time in their country home. Occasionally I brought the boys to the apartment for the weekend, where Philippe accepted them through the half-open door as if I'd come to deliver a package. They were swallowed by a luxurious black hole.

He did come to my room once and took the papers from on top of the wobbly wardrobe—the mountain of dust I had never touched. I could imagine him sitting there while I was at work in his wife and children's new home, standing at my window looking at the unchanged view. A visitor to his own history.

Though unpleasant, it didn't scare me. In exchange, I told myself, I had been given a story I was now writing out bit by bit in a new graph-paper notebook. Ostensibly to practice my French. It was a story I could tell Clara, picking elements from a grab bag of anecdotes, astonished by the violence that had taken place here so recently in places we knew, where we had bought things or at least walked by. *Imagine we'd been here three or four years ago.* . . . We appropriated the coordinates of the drama. I enjoyed completing it, linking the points he'd provided. Filling the gaps and fleshing out events, bringing to life a girl who had written her name on the wall here in the not-so-distant past.

Maybe it helped me to understand what you did a little better, Flo. Which is not to say I forgave you. Philippe had given me his story on his own initiative, and the giving made the exchange a completely different thing. Completely different.

WHEN I FLICKED ON the light, I saw that Philippe had been in the room again. A few loose sheets of paper were on the table, my table, A5. The paper had a letterhead and must have come from his father's supply. Emblazoned across the top in dark-blue italics it said *M.C. LAMBERT, DIRECTEUR, DIRECTION GÉNÉRALE DES TÉLÉCOMMUNICATIONS*, with the pointy logo of La Poste beneath it. His father had retired in 1970 and died in 1988; the company had been privatized as France Télécom. The paper, at least twenty years old, no longer represented anything but had been kept all the same, just as families like the Lamberts kept every crumb that confirmed their status. There were series of numbers scribbled on it. Numbers I couldn't make any sense of—calculations perhaps, dates, amounts? Philippe must have jotted them down, the handwriting seemed familiar from notes I'd seen around the apartment— until recently. I swept the sheets of paper together and put them in the box.

Not much longer and my work would be done. The past few months had been pressed together like the bellows of an accordion. A new au pair had been found, a Flemish girl with a painter's name, Berthe. I didn't want to and couldn't think about what would happen next; mostly I tried to banish thoughts of my imminent parting from Louis.

ON WEDNESDAY, JUNE 27, 1990, I saw Philippe once again. It was easy to look up the date because of the exceptional weather. After a few warm weeks the sky over Paris turned a bilious yellow, then ashen. The walls I was working between were sweating, the banisters were sticky, the city was simmering. Laurence's flights had been canceled because of the predicted storm, she was in the apartment and had sent me home as soon as I'd picked Nicolas up from school. My having to cross half the city in that same predicted storm was beyond her powers of imagination; as far as that went, nothing had changed.

Holding a newspaper over my head, I'd walked down the streets to the Metro, the paper saturating and turning to gray sludge in less than a minute. Water was rushing through the gutters. Crashing thunder followed almost immediately upon lightning bolts that reduced the street to two-dimensional black and white. Nobody who reached the Metro was dry, the cars filled with steaming bodies whose decorum dripped off and gathered in puddles on the studded flooring. Wet hair, sopping shoes, clothes stuck to bodies; even the stoic French were defeated.

Halfway along line 1, under the Champs-Élysées, the train's interior lights started flickering. The train slowed, stopped, hiccupped, started moving again slowly, and finally crept into George V station. Over a blaring intercom, passengers were requested to leave the station in a calm and orderly fashion, the Metro was no longer running "due to weather conditions." The station lights were flickering too, the floors wet and slippery, people lost their footing and screamed. The escalators were out of order, the wet crowd jostled up the stairs. The turnstiles were all wide open and it was only approaching the exit that we fully understood what was going on: The water was now gushing down the steps. Paris was drowning and the Metro stations were filling up like the city's drains. Brown water ran over my feet as I worked my way up, clinging to the banister while other wet bodies thronged around me. After emerging on the avenue, people fled into the Monoprix or shot down a side street in search of a brasserie or some other open door.

Shivering now, with the heat washed away completely, I started walking home. The Arc de Triomphe rose behind the veil of rain like a hazy monolith. Cars and vans were throwing up screens of water around the entrances to the traffic circle. Water was flowing off the intersection and gushing down Avenues Marceau, d'Iéna, Kléber, Victor Hugo, all rivers I had to wade. The traffic lights had died. I tried my luck at the crosswalks while the storm kept stirring the black sky and the thunder pealed. I ran past the dripping trees on Avenue Foch, heading downhill, downstream toward my neighborhood, whose haughty opulence seemed even more absurd in these circumstances. The streetlights had failed, the whole neighborhood was unlit. The beige, now dark yellow facade of the outer blocks rose up like a wall of death masks. I ran, wet to the skin, my flip-flops lost somewhere along the way, ice-cold feet splashing on the submerged sidewalks. I ran and ran, past the embassies, past the glossy wrought iron gates with black nameplates on them, another black wall. There was my side street, there was my street, there was my door, another dark hole without electricity, a code lock, or light, but with the concierge on the lookout, a real role at last in this emergency, the guardian of her fortress. *Entrez, entrez, ma petite.* I slithered into the lobby like a fish.

Philippe hadn't gone into my room this time but was waiting for me at the servant's entrance to his mother's apartment, halfway up the spiral staircase. I was wet, chilled to the bone, and barefoot, but he didn't seem to notice. He was smoking in the open doorway, a half-filled ashtray on the floor. He'd been standing there awhile. He wanted to say goodbye to me, he said. He was sorry that he'd been in my room, he was sorry if he'd given me a fright, he was sorry . . . He was sorry about everything.

Doesn't matter, I said, teeth chattering. I wanted to dry off, I wanted to get away, suddenly I knew that I wanted to be gone. It was over. Louis would forget me; at most I'd be a vague patch in his infant brain, overwritten by all the things he was going to experience. Clara would stay a friend, if we both made more of an effort and if she didn't die so young—things that were still inconceivably distant in a hazy new century. Paris would remain a part of me. I would take the language with me like a diamond I had single-handedly dug from a mine. I would write down the stories—maybe. I wouldn't look back. And you, Flo, were further away than ever. You had become that pebble in my shoe, and I wasn't even wearing shoes on my cold, clammy feet. I had started a new story.

"You took good care of my sons," he said. "I wanted to thank you for that."

I nodded.

"Tomorrow I'm going to a clinic. There's a treatment . . ." The white of his eyes was showing like an animal's. "There is a treatment. I have to try it." Yes, maybe there was. The girl had been sent back to her mother in Tübingen and that was an end to it, but not all victims are equal. For a Lambert there would always be another treatment, a clinic, a doctor, new developments, improvement perhaps. I thought of the two little boys, their brown eyes, their little hands, and hoped very much that the treatment would help.

"I enjoyed working with your family," I said.

"There is one thing, Marie," Philippe said. "There are things I've seen. . . . I feel the rustling around you. I don't know what it is about you, why you came here. . . . Things are going to happen. Not with you, but around you. You have to be careful. It is still very unclear, you understand, I've tried to pinpoint the day. I couldn't. But I know it doesn't end here. And that you mustn't be there."

I didn't understand, I was very cold.

"It's not going to stop. I wrote things down, maybe you saw them."

I had. The sheets of paper.

"But I can't work out when. All I know is that you have to watch out for the thirteenth."

"The thirteenth?"

"The thirteenth. Friday the thirteenth."

THE *THIRTEENTH?* THAT WAS what he had to tell me? *Friday the thirteenth?*

Yes. That was what he said, Flo.

"SORRY. THE THIRTEENTH. I know, that's something for old wives, children, fairy tales. Black cats. Horoscopes." He shrugged. "I can't see it any other way, Marie, the only warning I have is for the thirteenth," he said. "On Friday the thirteenth, you have to stay put. Above all, you mustn't want to be somewhere else."

I could hardly contain my laughter. And I wanted to get away, to run up the stairs. He was really, absolutely, stark raving mad. Friday the thirteenth. And he was Jesus, I suppose. And the flood was coming; more to the point, it had started today.

He turned away with a shrill gasp.

"You don't believe me, Marie. I know that expression. The look they always give me. Forget it. But not completely. Think about it when you need to. It's going to take a long time. Long enough to . . ."

To what?

"Long enough to forget and then remember it again."

. . .

HE TOOK MY HAND, his burning hand around my cold fingers, and shook it as if I'd just concluded a job interview.

"Good luck with your . . . with the treatment," I said. He shuffled back and closed the door and I walked up the stairs to my room.

It was the last time I saw him.

V

Flo's Story

2015

YOUR YEARS HAVEN'T BEEN my years, Flo, but they'll have this in common: a mixture of the banal and the exceptional. What remains probably resembles all those photos you kept on your shelf back then, not special but unrepeatable.

My father is holding a grandchild and looking up at the camera like a young man I've never seen before. My mother is waving from the doorway of the apartment, wearing a red cardigan that stands out against the yellow door and the glazed blue flowerpot on the walkway. The black doorjamb behind her completes the Mondrian, and that, black-white-blue-yellow-red, is the last picture of her that exists. The photos were taken with a disposable camera by my middle sister; at the time I was still holding firm to my resolution to never take photos of people again.

Our parents disappear in the pre-euro days, too soon and almost together. They leave before the distance between us has grown large enough for us to reconcile ourselves to our childhood. Too soon to get to know them as people, not just as parents.

For months after clearing out their apartment, I feel an unexpectedly keen longing for their filter coffee, their tiny entrance hall with the beveled mirror, their wood-chip wallpaper, and the accompanying feeling of wanting to run away from that forever. I even miss their view of the parking lot, and the balcony railing with the big fat plastic crow on it, which they only acquired after the three of us had left home. We sisters take one photo album each and promise to swap them regularly.

SEEN FROM ABOVE, EVERYTHING in a life really is a banal story that follows a pattern. After Paris, back to the Netherlands. A teaching degree, high school French. Rushing to settle down, suddenly having kids, who are so extraordinarily new and unburdened. Vacations, work, catching the same train every day. Call it a rut if you will, call it security. Another part of the country, more space. Eyes that look up from a screen (all at once there are screens everywhere) and disrupt everything. Development and death coinciding. A house with a red roof and a magnolia in the front yard. Worries. Solutions.

But even this flyover is none of your business, Flo. I think that's enough.

IN THE INTERVENING YEARS I never once looked inside your book. It did well, otherwise I wouldn't have encountered it so often in bookstores in the photography sections I still scanned out of habit. If I saw it, I ignored it. Something in me was still expecting to be addressed, recognized, asked, Was that you? No, that wasn't me, I would say. No. What makes you think that? No, no idea. No. I was ready and waiting until I was sure that every external similarity had disappeared, but the question never came. The one time I picked up the white book with the M. on the spine in a secondhand bookstore, it was to put it unopened at the bottom of a pile where nobody would see it.

THE GRAPH-PAPER NOTEBOOKS AND the contact sheets and the loose pages turn up now and then, when moving, or clearing out a cupboard. Then I'd pick up the dry paper from the previous century and feel it between my fingertips before putting it back.

THE THINGS IT CONTAINED belonged to a period that was only significant for me, a scrap of evidence that these things had happened, or at least that I had experienced them. The odd jotting here and there, a notebook, contact sheets, a few loose pages—all in all, it was a rather slim account of events (memoirs, nothing but the "charnel house of truth," according to the Goncourt brothers—and who still knows who they are? I tell my current students and have to explain the terms *memoir* and *charnel house* before we even get to the forgotten writers). But for me it was enough; I only needed to touch the papers and, like unfolding maps opening out one after the other, the entire episode rose before me as a fragile construction of light and shadow, filling the room to the ceiling, pressing against the windows, flimsy and transparent, only visible to me, but allowing me, if I looked closely, to see my younger self walking, searching, climbing stairs, passing the swinging doors, finding my way. One sigh and everything collapsed back to that little pile. I kept it in that old box with the lid shut, the plastic a little harder and a little more yellowed now, and a size that was discontinued so long ago I could never find one that stacked on top of it. Throwing it out would have been an easy, casual act, but I didn't do it. Paris was my rock bottom, the bare soil you instructors talked about, perhaps. Carrying it around with me felt right, wherever I went and without any members of the family I acquired asking about it; meaningless to everyone else, but for me, the evidence that it was possible to progress under your own steam.

IT COULD HAVE STAYED like that, Flo. But you have your reasons for having listened until now to the files I've been dictating for you and sending from Paris, one installment after the other. I'm not finished yet. I did tell you that every story rests on three points, remember?

AN ASSISTANT POSED THE question in the fall of 2015. Florence da Silva is inviting me to a photography fair, Paris Photo, where a reissue of *The Making of M.* will be presented. The assistant is glad to have been able to track me down. It will be an honor to welcome me, the book's source of inspiration, to Paris for the festive presentation and a "private encounter beforehand." Travel expenses and a hotel for two nights will be reimbursed.

After a bottomless silence for a quarter of a century, this proposal almost makes me vomit. Fortunately, nobody's home. I put the dog on the leash and go walking. I walk straight out the front door of our house, all the way to the mudflats and back. The dikes and the vast sky keep their secrets.

It's only when I can look at the invitation without feeling sick that I see the date. A lukewarm stream rises from the soles of my feet, filling me to every extremity. I go up to the attic, get out the box, and sit for a while with it on my knees, breathing in the old smell. I don't need to spread out the pages to know that somewhere under the letterhead with that pointy logo, among the other numbers, the correct date will be written. This must be it.

AND SO, WE ARRIVE at the day. November 13, 2015. The day that popped into Philippe Lambert's head, along with so many other possibilities. He scribbled the combinations of numbers down at the table in my room. I pictured his ballpoint floating over the numbers like a divining rod. Maybe he wanted to cross some out, but in the end he left them all. I thought at the time he'd gone mad. Not dangerously mad, but gradually coming off the rails, a slowly but surely derailed madman. Cuckoo. The commemoration in Rue de Rennes had apparently been the final straw, though I hadn't noticed that at the time. Let's not forget that I was only twenty-one, *not as young as the other girls*, but still—so young.

There are many pictures of that thirteenth, but what good are they to you? What do they say? I wasn't able to prevent anything, Flo, I wasn't able to divert anything. The idea that it might've been possible to do that ultimately cost Philippe everything. Prevention, no, but re-creating that day is something I can do. I will build it up for you in words. This is how it must have gone.

⌒

YOU LEAVE FOR PARIS on a sunny Friday morning, November 13, 2015. Even in Rotterdam, where you board the Thalys, it's already shaping up to be an exceptionally mild autumn day. A beam of low morning sunlight pierces the damp air under the large roof.

You haven't taken the first train, why would you? Arriving in Paris around noon, walking out of Gare du Nord, and crossing the road to lunch in Terminus Nord—a half dozen oysters and glass of Sancerre, followed by steak tartare, that's the plan. Some scenarios are just too good not to follow. You have a small case with you and a light yellow sling bag made of soft calfskin and you're wearing cowboy boots, of course. You no longer have irons nailed to the heels and toes, you left that habit behind in the nineties, but the boots remain. They're new, ocher with brown stitching. You love the extra height and authority they give you. You love the sound of the solid heels as you cross the station concourse, the way they ring out despite the surrounding racket. You're still tall, people glance your way as you pass. Pushing sixty, but besides some crow's feet, you seem immune to time. Your curls, kept shoulder length for years, are graying sensationally. Another year or two and they'll be completely white. It will soften your olive face.

When you were approached by a publisher of photography books two years ago, a trip like this was something you could never have suspected. The publishing house was called Mnemosyne, the goddess of memory. That reference appealed to you. Isn't that what photos do, anchor memory? Shape it, even? Because a situation disappears as soon as a photo of it exists, engulfed and replaced by the captured image. That was why you had always placed so much emphasis on seeing, so that your students began with an awareness of what they were recording, the story that would be fixed in the photograph, realizing their task and the power they wielded over reality. That is still the case. Maybe even more than before, when there were so many fewer images and more gaps for imagination to fill.

Ton Helder, the publisher, really made a project of you. First, your early books published as facsimile editions, and your three books from the 2000s collected in cheaper but still attractive volumes. For your last book, from just 2012, he commissioned an external picture editor to give it a completely new layout. It was an unbelievable boost for the photos, that outsider's perspective. The picture editor, a smart millennial with a cleft lip, had the decisiveness of someone who has always had to fight that little bit harder. Zilver was her name, you must have found that amusing. In the ten years you lived together, your partner sometimes fantasized about a daughter he wanted to call Silver—Silver da Silva, what could be more beautiful than that? But you didn't want children, out of the question. The whole concept of reproduction had never appealed to you, there were other ways to live on.

Your collaboration with Zilver was so successful that she was now working on a retrospective. She'd been through your archives like a medic doing triage under fire: These photos are keepers, these ones need work, dump them. It was going to be a coffee table book, magnificently printed, available on subscription only. This presentation in Paris was the prelude.

You think of Robbie for a moment as you lower yourself onto the Thalys seat—first class, still a bit cramped, but at least they bring you coffee. The contact with the new publisher and picture editor had been *the* moment to definitively dial back your collaboration with Robbie. He still produced the most beautiful handmade prints in all of Europe, but as an assistant for field-work he wasn't much use. He'd got messy, forgetting appointments. For years now, he'd been drinking too much. The new collaborations had hurt, supplanting him. But Christ, after a quarter of a century . . . Not everyone has the capacity to reinvent themselves. You have to do what you have to do. He didn't need to move out. You're not cruel.

"WE'RE GOING TO RELAUNCH you at Paris Photo 2015," your publisher, Ton, said over coffee at your second meeting, while sliding a contract under your nose. "Florence, I have faith in this. Look at how well Ed van der Elsken's work is doing. It's on the way up again now for the third time. It should have happened a lot earlier, your former gallery owner and that Mickey Mouse publisher really missed an opportunity." He would take over both roles; that suited his broad view of the profession, more an agent than a publisher.

A "pragmatic groupie," that was how Ton Helder characterized himself—it had to be good and it had to sell. Your series of photos were conceived and made as books; as books he would help them back into the world. That was where the money was, and that was how to reach the public. *Many a mickle makes a muckle,* he'd learned that in America. So: Sell books, as many as possible. But as a publisher-slash-agent he had to think of both ends of the market. So sell photos too: Original 1980s prints were shooting up in price, that was favorable. Reprints as well, but then very large format and a very small print run. It was time for a TV appearance. "Your age," said Ton, "is an asset." Your stoic inaccessibility too, but he didn't say that out loud.

This was the trajectory: In 2015 we go big at Paris Photo; summer 2016, Les Rencontres d'Arles. From there, straight to the Armory in New York; that tandem always delivers. Partly the same buyers, the repetition pulls them over the line. Then deluxe editions in 2017 or 2018. Ton had a good line to the curator at the Stedelijk Museum in Amsterdam. He'd do some groundwork to get Hripsimé on board for a presentation to coincide with the release of the retrospective, he liked his chances.

"Female photographers are on the up, Florence. We're going to see that in the next few years. New appreciation for Nan Goldin, Bertien van Manen. Vivian Maier, you know, the posthumously discovered nanny with camera—the negatives-in-the-old-suitcase story—sells like hotcakes. Those prints are already unaffordable. The time's ripe and we can demonstrate how you paved the way for the new generation here in Europe." Ton could gild the lily sometimes, but his business sense was impeccable.

"In the Netherlands, anyway. I can defend the claim that you smoothed the way for Viviane Sassen, or Hellen van Meene, of course. Even Rineke Dijkstra . . ."

"Rineke is my generation, Ton," you said.

"I know. Doesn't matter. The point is, you've been here all this time and your photos, your method, is very now. Voyeuristic, but also anthropological and deeply humane. The Sophie Calle of the Low Countries, but with much better photos. There's kind of a connection to social media too, I think. That's what we're going to tell the world."

You nodded, and after reading the contract, you signed it. Ton hadn't lied, he kept his eye on the ball and lived up to everything he promised.

. . .

IT'S AN IDEA OF Zilver's: inviting the subjects of the photos to attend the presentation in Paris. The publisher is prepared to splash out on accommodation and travel costs; a live appearance by these people can contribute to the formation of the myth Ton mentions so often. Myths don't just arise spontaneously, you make them. Zilver does some prep: An hour's googling is enough to track down virtually all of the contacts. She sets up a Facebook account for you so that you can be found too and puts a few messages on it.

It's not really a success. The Antwerp rabbi has died, you hadn't expected anything else. Doreen has been back in the US for two decades now, she's been divorced twice in the meantime, and it's questionable whether this is something she wants to look back on at all; but that can wait till the Armory.

The twins from your fourth book are found. One of them, the younger by eight minutes, is going to Paris tomorrow. There's nothing left of his youthful beauty; the contrast between the angel in the photos and the fortysomething blob will be . . . interesting. He's looking forward to it and will bring his husband with him, he writes in an email that arrives almost immediately. The veteran from your sixth book has let you know that he wants to be left in peace, and Zafira (from *Unveiled*, your last book, from 2012) says that she is now "in a different phase."

The jackpot would be the presence of M., Marie. She didn't react to Zilver's email, after that you tried yourself. It's long ago, deep in the previous century. When Zilver shows you M.'s Facebook page, with just a few vague group photos on it, you have trouble picking her out. She is fuller and more feminine than you remember, it means nothing to you. You're better off looking at your own photos to summon up her face, a young face that could still go in any direction. And that angular body, that timid way of walking. It fascinated you at the time; she seemed so malleable. *The Making of M.* was undoubtedly your most complicated project, but also your most successful; you owe most of your modest reputation to that book. Never equaled either, but you've got over that frustration. Not many artists manage to make a potential classic, Ton said, and he was right.

YOU KNOW THAT M. didn't take it well back then, but that wasn't something you dwelled on. No time. You already had a new plan up and running, and teaching kept you busy as well. A few dents and dings are part of growing up, you can't be blamed for that. You put a lot of energy into M., a massive contribution to her artistic education, she knew so little. Those telephone conversations were too much, you wouldn't do that now, but what the hell. There are so many things that aren't allowed anymore—does that make them unethical retrospectively? It was the eighties. A different era.

You send her an email as one middle-aged woman to another, even if the other is a little younger. Your request is well considered and respectful. You formulate it precisely, saying that you're also curious about how M. experienced it. You talk about a vulnerable period in everyone's life, coming of age, how compared to now those years were much less public. What photography meant at the time. How you would do things differently now. You invite her to be present in Paris, which she probably knows much better than you—remembering just in time that she left for that city after rather abruptly dropping out of art school. You write that you'd like to look back together on "a turbulent period" that was so formative, "also for me." "Perhaps we can raise a glass to it together," you write. "I think that would be very special." You make a big departure from your usual practice by adding your number at the bottom of the email.

You're piqued when she doesn't reply. You send another message on Messenger and encourage Zilver to look for alternative addresses. She turns up a high school where M. teaches, near Groningen—of course, some people end up in places like that too. You send an email to her work address, not a peep from there either. After three unanswered attempts you give up. Take it or leave it.

ON THE THALYS, THE systems are in disarray because of the sudden warm weather—the heating is going full blast, but with the sun on the windows, air-conditioning would be more appropriate. You have laid your reading glasses and telephone on your lap, you close your eyes. You're free of all responsibilities. Mnemosyne has taken care of everything, you don't even have to concentrate on the schedule. The publishing house was able to do the opening on Wednesday and the first full day themselves. Ton knows you loathe ceremony and has arranged things just the way you like them. This afternoon you'll pop into the Grand Palais to view the stand and stroll around the fair a little. The intended private encounter with your main characters has been canceled because of the no-shows— it doesn't matter, one of the twins is coming tomorrow. You've kept this evening for yourself; they know how important that is to you. Tomorrow in the daytime, you'll take part in a panel discussion for Paris Photo Platform about "photography in relation to the book." You sighed, you can still only bear company in small doses and preferably self-selected. Ton said, "Just do this one." Meeting important people, sitting at a table with Nan Goldin, artist in focus at the fair and one of your heroes, even if you're almost the same age—it really is a good idea. Then the exclusive presentation of the stand, a VIP party, dinner with guests, the photo curator of the Pompidou . . . Your moment will come on Saturday evening; from now on it's one long descent toward it, gently rocking.

Antwerp and Brussels pass after you've fallen asleep. Somebody takes away the empty coffee cup and puts the table up. Gently shaking your shoulder when the train has passed the suburbs of Paris and entered the deep groove between tall buildings that leads to the station. When you walk out of Gare du Nord and onto the renovated square, it's a sunny sixty degrees. You unbutton your coat. An exceptionally beautiful November day, even the French think so.

⌒

THEY'VE BOOKED A ROOM for you at Hôtel du Prince Eugène on Boulevard Voltaire in the 11th arrondissement; a slightly less busy part of town and close to a convenient Metro station, Nation. The hotel has been recently renovated in a neobaroque style. The room is tiny but the bed is long enough. A bit on the dark side— with its anthracite-colored tiles, the bathroom makes you think of a tomb—but it's at the back and quiet and you like that. The lunch was excellent, you're glowing. You take off your rings and wash your hands, freshen yourself up, rub Lancôme (always Lancôme) on your skin, which is feeling dry after traveling, and put all five of your silver rings back on, covering the white circles on your fingers. You slip on a light silk blouse that survived the trip rolled up tightly in your suitcase and pull a cognac-colored jacket on over it. You leave on your narrow-legged jeans and don't need to think about your shoes. If the reproductions in the stairwell are to be trusted, Prince Eugène was an emaciated man with a remarkably long nose, who defeated the Turks in the Battle of Zenta. The small Maghrebi at reception swipes up the jangling keys you deposit on the counter without meeting his eye. His "Bonne soirée, madame" dies on the carpet of the lobby while you stroll out. Now you're leaving the dark hotel, you notice the exuberant light again, so strange in combination with the bare trees.

THERE ARE LOCATIONS THAT are hard to take in at a single glance, and the Grand Palais is one of them. The interior under the glass dome is immense. More than a hundred years after its construction, the roof still seems like a structural impossibility. It's almost five, the sky over Paris is turning orange, giving a Mediterranean glow to the whole exhibition area. It's your first time inside. Under the dome, Paris Photo extends like a horizontal doll's house—intimate as you walk through it, a jumble of poky little spaces when viewed from above. The tinted daylight hangs over it like a disorienting haze. First, you take the time to stroll around the long, high gallery, looking down at the stands. All that ambition, bathing in halogen spotlights. It's nice to no longer be so very young. Ton is right, your age is an advantage, it makes a fair like this less emotionally charged. You rest your elbows on the wrought iron balustrade, studying the map and the view below until you've localized Mnemosyne close to the outside edge, in the row of "international publishers." It's a substantial stand; from this distance you recognize the large prints of your own photos and the balding pate of Ton, who is gesturing enthusiastically as he explains something to a woman in sunglasses.

REACHING THIS MOMENT OF the day, I wish I'd tried to call you, Flo. But I didn't and you would probably have ignored an unknown number. In any case, there are no messages when you pull out your phone at five to take a photo of the view of the fair from above and send it to Robbie.

Ton and Zilver greet you at the stand with a brief hug. How was your trip? Yes, it's warm, how nice you're here, no, it's fantastic, look at those stickers, we've sold so much, yes, books too, a junior curator from MoMA came by, who knows, it's going smoothly.

Seeing your own work this big around you is dissociative, as if it's not yours, but you don't let it show. There are the twins, printed as life-size photo wallpaper for the stand, posing in a corner by the bookcase in your house, the house you still own. There is an extensive series of small prints from *Days with Doreen*, which always touches a chord and sells well. First-time buyers in particular love that sleek American lifestyle, Ton says, the 1950s aesthetics of one of those compounds. He's right, there are little orange stickers almost everywhere, sometimes a few in a row. The focus of the presentation is on *The Making of M.*, which, according to Ton, still has the potential to become a Dutch *Love on the Left Bank*. Or at least like that book about Amsterdam, Ed van der Elsken's other classic—that category is definitely within reach, he says. The reissue looks fabulous—even the white linen cover matches perfectly, it's unbelievable how well they do that these days. They've stacked them in twisted columns, with an open copy of the English edition in a Perspex stand on top of each column.

On the wall are four tall, narrow prints from the sequence of M. coming out through her front door, four moments over the course of a year, perhaps one and a half, 1988 to 1989. Taken from across the road. Robbie spent a lot of hours on it, remember? Fabulous photos. Always that same listless, no, wary way of stepping down onto the sidewalk. As if she's about to feel the water of a swimming pool, her shoulders slightly rounded. Unmistakably the same girl, despite the transformation of her appearance. M. becomes slighter, skinnier, her face more triangular, the nondescript boyish hair grows out; she starts wearing it long with straight bangs. The cheekbones catch the light. In the last photo she's wearing a leather coat you gave her. The new look, meant to be arty, doesn't sit comfortably on her. You'd hoped for a Nico-like development, something enigmatic, but most of all she radiates insecurity, and ultimately that's even better, the quality that made the book a success at the time and still can now.

You know why Ton has had these photos blown up like this and hung them so prominently. When it comes down to it, everyone sees a reflection of themselves growing up. It's the difficult metamorphosis that appeals, from teenager to young woman, here clearly on the wrong track. Whether people looked at them in the 1990s, the 2000s, the 2010s, even now—these photos still have that effect.

A skinny staff member from Paris Photo breezes into the stand. Lanyard, lipstick, an armful of brochures. The habit of women in the cultural sector to immediately present themselves as an intimate friend has caught on in France too. Beaming, she comes straight up to you, holds out a small, cold hand and introduces herself in a hoarse voice as Claudine. Perfume and a waft of cigarette smoke; the smokers' emergency exit can't be far. "Florence! *Enfin!* It's such an honor to meet you! Claudine, *enchantée!*" Claudine is going to be accompanying you tomorrow, she says, it will be such an exciting day, *tout* Paris Photo is looking forward to the conference. She is sure that *Nan-e Goldin-e* and Florence will have so much to discuss. And after that, the festive *présentation*, there will undoubtedly be a lot of interest. The Netherlands is such a rich country for photography, truly *extraordinaire*, and it is so special to meet someone who has been a part of that for so long. . . . The gap between her front teeth makes her look somehow childish. Champagne arrives from somewhere, you're given a glass. You clink it against Ton's and Zilver's and smile along with everyone else, yes, it's going to be a festive weekend. The slight glow from lunch had faded but is now refreshed, you raise another toast. Then you excuse yourself by saying you'd like to visit the fair now while you have time for it. Ton and Zilver will be manning the stand until ten p.m., you really don't mind eating alone? No, not at all, you enjoy it, another moment for yourself. Your phone doesn't vibrate in your pocket, nothing disturbs the course of events.

YOU LEAVE THE GRAND Palais under an evening sky that has turned to velvet. Streetlights stand out against its deep purple like stars. It's an evening you couldn't capture on film; it would take a painter. You walk along Avenue Winston Churchill to the Champs-Élysées, where a few cars with German flags fluttering out of the windows drive past on their way to Place de l'Étoile for a few more turns around the Arc de Triomphe. France are playing Germany tonight in a friendly at the Stade de France, you heard that somewhere—or did you read it earlier in the Metro? On a billboard?

It's strange how information one is indifferent to invariably seeks one out, while signals that matter often go astray. In this way, a teenage couple you don't notice pass in the opposite direction. Their winter coats are hanging open to reveal sweatshirts with JE SUIS CHARLIE on the chest. A fresh print, the tourist edition. A bloody attack on the editorial office of the weekly *Charlie Hebdo* in January, now marketed as a souvenir that lets you flaunt your commitment with cool lettering. The two have their arms wrapped around each other's shoulders, on their way to hang a padlock on the Pont des Arts, not knowing that the mayor of Paris recently banned it, so they'll have to find another location. She runs her fingers through her blue hair, the piercings in her eyebrows glint under the streetlights, and she pulls her boyfriend toward her greedily. They kiss and laugh, top of the world. In a couple of hours, they will mark themselves as safe on their social media profiles and no longer think about locks on bridges, just the train home. They'll never wear those sweatshirts again. You go into the Champs-Élysées–Clemenceau Metro station; despite its fancy name, a plain—even grim—station. Claudine is going to be totally exhausting tomorrow, you know that already.

⌐

IT'S QUARTER TO NINE when you sit down in the roofed sidewalk extension of Comptoir Voltaire, a brasserie on the corner next to your hotel. The ornate letters on the red awning proclaim *cuisine traditionnelle*—for a carnivore like you, places like this often turn out well. Inside there is a large screen, the soccer match is about to start. That's why you choose to sit behind the glass of the extension, in the intermediary zone. Not bothered by the TV screen inside and not bothered by the smokers in chairs on the sidewalk proper, on the busy boulevard. It's a neighborhood restaurant, people enter in small groups, talking as they come through the swinging doors, and you only hear French around you. A buzz of language you don't need to follow. The tables around you fill up, you arrived just in time.

Inside, the French and German anthems play, a waitress brings you the menu and makes a remark you don't quite follow about the match. "Oh, excuse me, I thought you were French," she says, smiling, and returns in no time with a tall glass of wheat beer, as requested. CATHÉRINE is written on the brass nameplate pinned to her white blouse. A woman who understands her profession; you immediately feel at ease. *Viande?* The young woman recommends the sirloin steak with mustard sauce—with charcuterie from Auvergne as a starter, perhaps? It's their specialty.

I WASN'T SUPPOSED TO move on the thirteenth, I wasn't supposed to be anywhere else and now you are there. I should have paid more attention, I should have texted you. A message you would now hear coming in, that you would open to read: "Flo, a message from M. It is not a good day to be there. Phoned you, you didn't answer. Should have warned you sooner. Try to leave the city. Get away from there." Better still if I used all caps.

But I don't. I'm home, far away up north. It's a Friday the thirteenth and I don't do anything. That's a fact.

YOU HEAR YOUR PHONE buzz and fish your reading glasses out of your calfskin bag to read it. A message from Zilver: "Twin canceled for presentation tomorrow. Food poisoning. Doesn't matter, will be fantastic anyway. Enjoy your evening, *à demain!*"

Your thumb floats over the screen; should you react? It's annoying, but also a relief. You weren't looking forward to the dutiful small talk with a former subject. You frown, put your glasses back on, take them off again.

"Mauvaise nouvelle, madame?" A man in a suit on your right has spoken to you. Dark brown eyes, short graying hair, a handsome man who's just come from work. Like you, he's folded up at his small sidewalk table. You recognize each other the way tall people recognize each other everywhere.

"*No, it's nothing,*" you say. "*It's, um . . . just somebody I used to know who canceled an appointment.*" A pop song from a few years ago occurs to you, "Somebody That I Used to Know," you remember quite liking it, for new music. You lower your guard for this man. And why not?

"*A disappointment?*" His English is beautiful.

"*No, not really,*" you say. "*It's all so . . . long ago.*" You smile; anything could happen tonight—it's been a while since you had that feeling.

"*Let me guess,*" the man says, "*maybe that person is superstitious and doesn't like Friday the thirteenth?*" He counts his attempts, first the pinkie, now the ring finger. "*Or maybe he doesn't realize quite how charming his former acquaintance is?*"

He's direct, you don't mind that. He's wearing a wedding ring, that's his business.

"*We'll drink to that,*" you say, and raise your glass.

"*Nelson,*" he says.

"*Florence,*" you say, and slip your phone back into your pocket. When it vibrates again, you ignore it. The charcuterie arrives.

THERE ARE SO MANY moments that can be identified as the starting point for this night, unfortunately, your night too, Flo. The lead-up began so long ago, years ago, maybe decades ago, yes, decades ago, long before the birth of the men who are now preparing their attack. The signing of treaties, the occupation of territories, France taking the side of Iraq . . . But that's something for analysts, later. As always, we are blind and deaf as we move through the time that envelops us. When the bomb went off in Rue de Rennes, Philippe Lambert had no insight into the whys and wherefores. The Berlin Wall fell and I thought it had happened suddenly, for no reason; history always feels like that. For tonight, in the story of this evening, let's take a literal starting shot.

It's quarter past nine when a loud bang sounds in the stadium. As if someone managed to smuggle in some powerful fireworks. Among the spectators in the stadium, people watching in their living rooms and in the brasserie too, some people hear the shot, but as yet nobody suspects it for what it is. Yes, somebody says, see? Football is war.

The chants ring out, glasses are passed around. You're sitting in the sidewalk extension and don't hear a thing.

Four minutes later a more powerful explosion is heard in the Stade de France; this time player Patrice Evra, who has just got the ball, hesitates. He looks up at the stands, people look at the screen, where's it coming from? So loud!

This too is something you don't see, don't hear. But that's how it starts, how the wave rises. On the street in front of the stadium in Saint-Denis, a couple of miles north of the city, two men have blown themselves up. Outside the stadium on Avenue Jules Rimet, white fluff is floating down under the yellow streetlights, tufts of down, like snow, from the ripped coat of a man who thought he was gaining admission to paradise. Snow on a mild evening in November and then a wave through the city.

François Hollande, the president with the permanently disappointed expression, is pulled from the grandstand, informed, taken to safety.

Now four men in a black SEAT Leon and on a scooter set out, three with automatic weapons and one wearing an explosive vest, starting their journey through the "triangle of liberty"—Place de la Bastille, Place de la République, Place de la Nation—the symbolism has been drummed into them: Hit whatever you can within that triangle, everyone there is guilty, every bullet is good.

Now the telephone lines of the emergency services start glowing, now the gravity of the situation grips the firefighters and the nurses and the ER doctors and the paramedics who see not one, not two, not three, but a whole series of waves breaking on top of one another.

No, this is not an exercise.

One sidewalk café, another sidewalk café, an intersection behind the Saint-Louis hospital, two hundred yards from the ER. Fifteen dead. Another sidewalk café, shot up from the scooter: five dead. The targets are chosen based on accessibility, line of fire, chances of success. Every bullet has to count.

The car drives to a café across from a large women's branch of the Salvation Army. It's a café where birthdays are celebrated, where locals gather but also complain about the noise, where the chairs spread out too far across the sidewalk, where there's always a beggar going from table to table. In one and a half minutes, nineteen people are shot dead and the rest are crawling through the blood, holding the dying tight and trying to save limbs, eyes, hands.

The car drives farther to drop a man with an explosive vest off on Boulevard Voltaire, then continues to the concert venue a little farther along, where fifteen hundred people are unsuspectingly singing along to a garage band, their heads swaying in time under the colored lights. Ninety of them will not survive. The facts are cruel, Flo, but summing them up is the only way to tell this story.

And you're sitting there in that sunroom under the gas heater that casts a red glow on your curls and blurs the fine wrinkles on your and your charming neighbors' faces. You slide your plate to the edge of the small table, giving a sideways nod to the server. That was a good start, not excellent, but very good. "*How was yours?*" you ask the man next to you, who is no longer a stranger.

Neither of you thinks for a second about what's been placed on the scales that evening, the latest needle to be threaded with history's embroidery thread: French air support in Syria, or Islamic State, *Daech*, the French say. What could these enormous abstractions have to do with you? With him? With the others who will lose their lives or suffer injuries in the next few minutes?

I HESITATE, FLO. I now understand what Philippe meant when he said that foreknowledge is a curse. That you can't change the course of events, not even when you suspect what they might be. That you can't give someone a different life no matter how hard you try— you know that. Not ahead of time, not during, not retrospectively. You can't even make a life; it makes itself to everyone's surprise, it follows its own course. I'm not talking about fate—fate is a fabrication for the needy—but don't downplay the role of coincidence. Walking into a bar, meeting someone. Missing a bus or just making a train, not answering a question or picking up the phone, finding an ad with just the right number of words. Being born in a place where blood was shed, accepting an invitation, turning at the next corner instead of this one. Standing close to a tree that lightning will strike. Taking a photo or not, capturing something or letting it go. You think you can influence something, that resolute decisions will turn events in a certain direction, that they're controllable. Everyone tells everyone else that all the time—we are so desperate to have that power.

JUST AFTER TEN THIRTY, just after the sirloin steak has been placed in front of you with a supple gesture, a man comes into the sunroom.

He thinks he has to push, bumps into the door, then pulls it open a little too hard so that several people look up, you too, and you think, Take it easy, it's not a saloon.

A prematurely aged young man, with heavy eyes in a narrow face, dressed in a long black coat, takes two, three steps in. He brings fresh evening air and a whiff of cigarette smoke in with him from the sidewalk. He unbuttons his coat.

LATER THERE WILL BE witnesses who will say: He looked suspicious, nervous. Somebody else will state: He was very well groomed, as if he'd just come from the hairdresser's. In such an important moment there has to be something noticeable, if only in hindsight. But the truth is that nothing really registered with anyone, besides the door swinging open too violently. The waitress, Cathérine, walks up to the customer to welcome him and show him to a seat. He sits down and she pulls out the device to take his order.

AND YOU, BEHIND HER and to one side, see her healthy, muscular back stretching the fabric of her white blouse. Or do you see the look in the eyes of the man next to you who wishes you *bon appétit* and raises his glass again? Red wine, from the bottle of Beaujolais you are sharing. Technically it's impossible for you to see both, the white back to your left and the brown eyes and red glass catching the light to your right.

But who cares about the precise order if these are the last impressions your retina will ever process? They are the last two images you will ever see: sharp, bright, clear, and beautiful, with all the colors separated from one another so precisely. A loud bang, a white flash, and a massive pressure wave ends it.

SOUND, PICTURE, SMELL, SHAPE, everything lost.

Nothing remains in its original place, or will ever return to it.

⌒

IN THE PHOTOS I saw your boots. Your hair, your bag. The blood on the waitress's white blouse. I could imagine her name badge. On a telephone video I saw a rhythmic movement somewhere on the edge of the picture, the CPR being given in vain to the person who turned out to be the bomber. There are so many photos, so much video. Emerging not only the next day, but long afterward. Time kept coughing them up.

ONCE ELOÏSE SCHILLER, A girl with a name like a bonbon, had to get by with a measly five photos of the scene of the crime where she almost died. She lost her hearing and her ability to move smoothly there, but there isn't a trace of her to be found in a single photo.

Now it's incredible how much is visible, almost from second to second, sometimes from different angles. As if the plotters were already planning "the making of" along with their attack.

But some things don't change. You need to create a hierarchy to contain your thoughts, otherwise a catastrophe like this is beyond comprehension. A half hour, six locations, so many dead, so many wounded, a hostage situation, more dead; you need a timeline and a scale of magnitude and seriousness. The suicide attack on brasserie Comptoir Voltaire ends up at the bottom of the list of November 13, 2015. The only fatality is the bomber. His explosive vest only partially detonated, so it could have been worse, they say. The wounded are counted and recounted and recorded but, as usual, they are overshadowed by the dead.

And by the survivors who miraculously come through this hell unscathed. Phoneless, shoeless, and clueless, but otherwise in one piece, they suddenly find themselves a couple of streets removed from the scene. Blown there in terror, friends lost, confused, born naked on a sidewalk in a city they only visited for an evening out.

Unharmed survivors who are cared for by strangers, brought in and sat down on the sofa, questioned in a foreign language: Who are you, what happened? Then again in another language, and then in sign language, and finally with a cup of tea. Those who have crept through the eye of the needle without a scratch, at least none that are visible on the outside (maybe they're angels), who find each other again after a couple of hours or days and are suddenly back home. Home. Where everything is the same and not at all. Where talk-show producers start calling them and following up with messages, because everyone wants to see an angel. Everyone wants to touch the survivor, everyone wants to hear them talk about it, everyone wants to know how bad it was, that there was a moment when the survivor thought, This is it—and then it wasn't. It's the law of the film script, and we love applying it to real-life events. Narrative documentary techniques.

But the wounded, the damaged don't talk. Or only years later. Or never.

IN THIS BRASSERIE 120 projectiles, bolts and screws, were removed from the furniture and the ceiling and the floor. From the waitress. From other people. And from you too. You get to keep your life, but you surrender your sight. In this place, you lose your eyes, your most important sense. And yes, Flo, that is horrific and I wish I could make it undone.

BUT NO MATTER HOW hard I try, whichever bits of the past I emphasize, whichever perspective I choose, that outcome is still fixed and you appear there, right on time. At that hour and in that place you could have avoided if someone on the street had kept you talking, if the traffic light had stayed red, or if another restaurant had appeared before you.

If I had placed more value on the improbable.

If I had warned you (but you wouldn't have listened, I know that for a fact).

If you'd received more, better, more urgent messages.

Or, going back to the beginning, if you had never cast your eye upon me in the first place.

⁓

THE TRIALS OF THOSE involved have started. Here in Paris there's no other news. They're the first item on every news bulletin, all the papers are covering them. Next week, back at school, I'll structure my lessons around them. Now I'm sitting at the window and looking out and naming things. There are some things you never unlearn.

ON THE OTHER SIDE of the road a zinc roof lights up in the late afternoon sun, a sun that's already casting long shadows. The roof, like all the roofs behind it, has a color that only exists here. An uncertain color, a blue that wants to be gray and a gray that wants to be blue. Sometimes the zinc matches the sky, in moments when it's about to rain. But now, against the clear dark blue of a September sky dotted with towering cumulonimbus clouds, the roofs stretch out as far as the eye can see, like an etched shingle beach. The building directly opposite is lower than this one, five floors and a courtyard. On the right a narrow section with eight dark-brown chimney pots rises above the roof. And farther along more earthenware chimney pots, and behind them even more; in a single field of vision I count forty-eight. Forty-eight households, who knows how many lives.

From where I'm sitting, at a table with a voice recorder into which I am dictating this last file, I can see into two apartments on the far side of the courtyard. On the left someone has closed the windows and curtains, but left the shutters open. Two planters

232 of SACHA BRONWASSER

contain the remnants of geraniums, dry and pale as paper. A glass jar next to them, wired to the railing, is half-full of cigarette butts. On the right, two windows are open. A boy in blue boxers wearing wireless earbuds is pacing back and forth on a parquet floor that shines like the deck of a ship, talking. He is young and muscular, but his shoulders are bent, like all young people's these days. (I've seen him twice downstairs locking his racing bike to the fence in the courtyard, between the other sports bikes that hang in a double layer off the railings there. He didn't notice me. I am the anonymous transient in the expensive Airbnb across from his apartment.)

The boy disappears from the frame of one window and reappears in the other, turns, disappears and emerges again. A little man in a weather house, only too young to know what that is. He gesticulates, slumps down on a burgundy sofa on the left, stands up again, appears on the right, and stands on the tiny balcony for a while with one leg raised, his bare toes curling around the ornate wrought iron balustrade. The white rods in his ears catch the light under his thick black hair. While talking, he runs his hand over his six-pack, scratches his ankle; his eyes wander over the courtyard and through the sky, he's in his head.

On the grayish-whitish-yellowish wall, the greige that also only exists here, a bundle of pipes bulges out between the two windows, protruding like intestines. The rainwater that has run down them over the years has left a trail on the stucco; it is the back of the young man's life.

Of course I see pigeons too, Flo, let's not forget them. They're always there. They appear on the left, shoot through the picture, disappear in the distance. A new flock comes from the right, the sun flashes briefly on their feathers as they turn, all at the same time.

The boy, his shoulders, the floor, the balustrade. The pipes from the wall between the windows, the bluish-gray, and the pigeons above it all.

It has been seen, it has been told, and now it exists.

Acknowledgments

My gratitude goes out to the people who asked, noticed, offered, and did the right things: Harold de Croon, Merel Bem, Hans Jansen, Jeroen Stout and Ineke Smits, Fiona Tan, Susanne Rudloff. This book wouldn't have been possible without you. Special thanks to David Colmer, who translated *Luister* into English with so much care, creativity, and elegance.

And I thank Paris, the inexhaustible.